Guy Stories

By Richard Beamish

Compiled by Kempton Dexter and Ron Kearse

Filidh Publishing

This is a PDF copy of
First Pocket Book Printing: 2021
ISBN 978-1-927848-65-4
Filidh Publishing
www.filidhbooks.com

Cover photograph by Ron Kearse.
Cover design by Danny Weeds

Richard Beamish

Richard Beamish was a long-time friend of ours, going back to the early 1980s. Even though he had a bit of a crusty exterior, he was actually very intelligent, sentimental and a loyal friend. He would always send us emails on International Friendship Day to remind us of how he valued the companionship of his friends.

Life led him on several international adventures, including teaching English in Pusan, South Korea, for a couple of years and then ending up in Budapest, Hungary. By then, he had met Aliz, the woman who became his Fiancé. He stayed with her for the last twenty years of his life.

He led a busy life in Budapest. When he wasn't teaching English, one could find him playing Squash regularly, and he became very active in the local chapter of Toastmasters. All the while, he continued to travel throughout Europe, ride his bicycle, write short stories, and he made a couple of attempts at writing novels too.

On December 8, 2020, a phone call from Budapest came through telling us of the shocking news that Richard had passed away. He was out riding his bike when he had a brain aneurysm and died immediately. That left us all (his friends) stunned! He was always there, and it seemed that he would always be there.

This is a collection of four short stories he wrote many years ago and sent them to us to look at, as he wanted to publish them as an anthology he called Guy Stories. With this small collection of his short stories, we celebrate Richard and the amazing friend he was. We honour his creativity, his compassion, and his quirky sense of humour.

This is for you, Richard. Wherever you are now, we hope that you can see that your stories are finally published, just as you had always wanted them to be.

Kempton Dexter
Ron Kearse

Table of Contents:

Melanie

His life changed after he met Melanie.

It happened on a hot summer's day. Stan had finished the watering and was culling daff and tulip bulbs behind the tool shed where a tall elm provided shade. He had laid planks on two sawhorses for a table to separate healthy bulbs from the rotten ones. The healthy bulbs were placed in wood flats, the discards in a wheelbarrow.

It was a tedious job that required only moderate attention and that, coupled with solitude, meant Stan was soon daydreaming about a girl he'd met in high school and hadn't seen since. Stan had a serious daydream habit. Sometimes he worried about losing his mind.

"I love your park," a woman said.

Stan stopped dead, turned around, and for the first time saw her.

She smiled. "Sorry for surprising you."

"No problem. I just never heard you coming."

She smiled again and waved an accusing finger. "You were daydreaming!"

She was tall and slender. Her long blond hair had wisps of grey. Her clothes looked fashionable and pricy. She was wearing sunglasses, a wedding ring, and Stan guessed she was probably forty.

"Yeah. I was lost in thought," he admitted. Stan was a touch over six feet and slim. He had brown hair, a beard, and was twenty-eight years old.

"Well, I just wanted to tell you how much I love your park, and I love the job you're doing here." Her voice was low, almost gravelly.

"Thanks a lot. I do my best. You must come here often."

"Almost every day. "

"I don't recall seeing you," said Stan.

She laughed. "Well, I've seen you."
She went and sat on a tree stump not far from where Stan was working.

"I hope you don't mind if I stay here and talk for a bit?"

"Not at all."

"How long have you worked here?" She had raised her knees and was hugging them with her arms.

"In this park, a year and a half, but I've been almost five years with Surrey Parks." Surrey was a suburb of Vancouver.

"You must like it."

"Yeah, it's good. Healthy, low stress, and the pay's not bad."

"What about those two over there?"

She was pointing at Fred and Agnes, the elderly homeless couple who lived in the park. They were sitting under a beech tree, their overloaded shopping carts nearby. Sometimes Stan helped them with government bureaucracy and even drove them to doctor's appointments. Otherwise, he kept his distance.

Stan chuckled and assumed a smile, hoping she wasn't yet another NIMBY asshole come to complain about Fred and Agnes. "Oh, Fred and Agnes. You don't need to worry about them. They wouldn't hurt a fly."

"Do they always hang out here?"

"More or less. Sometimes they disappear for a few days, but they always come back. Basically, they're either here or out picking bottles. Then they go to the liquor store and buy booze."

She released her knees and sat normally. "And why do they hang out here? I mean, don't people like that usually hang out in big city parks or live on the street?"

Stan nodded. "Good question. I've often wondered that myself. I guess it's because here they don't get hassled by other street people. Also, they like to hang out around the creek."

The creek was just west of the park. It was part of a five-acre wild space with coyotes, raccoons, deer, beaver, and even the occasional

9

bear. Although on municipal land, financial cutbacks meant it was largely abandoned. Sometimes the municipality cleared the beaver dams, but that was it. Rumour had it that a woman had been raped there, and few ventured in, Fred and Agnes being the exceptions.

"Do you know where they come from?" she asked.

Again, Stan nodded, wondering why she was interested in a couple of homeless drunks like Fred and Agnes.

"Nova Scotia. Believe it or not, they used to have regular jobs and a family, but they lost their house to the bank, and child welfare took their kids away. They're just a couple of hopeless lushes who don't cause any trouble." Stan decided to change the subject. "You live around here?"

"Pretty close. I come here when I go for a walk."

"I see." Stan glanced at his watch and smiled. "Almost quitting time. Do you have a job?"

She shook her head. "Nope. I'm a bored housewife with too much time on her hands."

Stan grinned. "These things happen."

He continued to pick through the bulbs; his hands were moist and slimy. He wondered what to say next, but she spoke first.

"My name's Melanie."

"I'm Stan."

Three days later, Stan and Melanie had their first date. Stan drove his Toyota pickup to the address she had given him and saw her waiting outside.

Melanie smiled and got in Stan's pickup. As before, she was casually yet expensively dressed: a sprinkling of jewelry, not too much makeup. A kind of athletic chic.

"So, this is where you live?"

Stan was asking about the one-storey house in front of where Melanie had been standing. Around it was a high white fence and a laurel hedge, and Stan could just make out the windows in which there were yellow curtains.

"That's it," said Melanie. "Home sweet home."

Stan shifted into first gear and began the drive to Vancouver.

Stan had decided to take Melanie to Queen Elizabeth Gardens, a jewel of the Vancouver Park Board. He knew the place well and had a friend who worked there. Also, he figured it was a good place for a first date, especially since Melanie seemed to like parks and gardens. They descended into the quarry and viewed the plants. Melanie showed polite interest, but when she saw some heather, she smiled, bent down, and plucked a leaf of the Winter Heath.

"Wow! Heather, I love it!"

"You must be Scottish," joked Stan.

Melanie blushed. "Actually, I'm Hungarian. My last name's Horvath."

"Is that your maiden name?"

"Nope. That's my real name. Melanie Horvath."

"I would have guessed Scottish."

In fact, there was something craggy and Celtic about Melanie, her face freckled, her eyes bright blue. She wasn't a natural blond, and her roots showed red. She didn't look like any Hungarian he had ever met.

After touring the quarry, Stan and Melanie went to the Queen Elizabeth Restaurant. They took a table by a window that offered a view of the West End, the harbour, and the mountains.

"Do you come from Vancouver?" asked Stan.

Melanie shook her head and perused the menu. "Not really…. We've moved around a lot. I've only been in Vancouver for eight months."

"And before that?"

"Like I said: we've moved around."

Stan let the matter drop. When the waitress came, he ordered lasagne with a vegetarian sauce and a cappuccino. Melanie, on the other hand, went all out.

"I'll have the lobster and a pasta salad. Plus, I'd like a bottle of French champagne." She paused, then said Veuve Clicquot with a terrible accent. "I'll have a peach and cottage cheese crepe for dessert."

Stan said nothing, but already he was calculating the price and whether he should ask Melanie to pay her share because, after all, he wasn't loaded. But then Melanie reached out, patted his hand, and smiled, "I'll get this."

Stan didn't quarrel, thinking she must have a rich husband. "Thanks a lot."

As they ate, Stan could tell that Melanie really got off on eating fine food, but not necessarily because it tasted good. Melanie was into luxury, the sheer thrill of buying expensive things. For her, lobster was a Rolls Royce, and champagne a Ferrari. The crepe was like a mink coat.

"Have some champagne," she offered.

Stan accepted one glass but refused the second. "I have to drive."

Melanie finished the bottle herself. Her face reddened, and she began to loosen up. She leaned forward, and under the table, her foot was touching his ankle.

"We can leave whenever you're ready," she said.

When the waitress arrived, Melanie paid with three one-hundred-dollar bills, leaving a very healthy tip.

On the way back, she insisted on buying more French champagne.

*

Like a lot of guys, Stan could count his women on both hands, and in his mind, Melanie had already become a cougar/vamp with a voracious appetite.

Arriving at Stan's place, she flung off her clothes and marched into the bedroom, and Stan quietly followed. Expecting a ferocious onslaught, Stan lay back and let her come at him, which she did. A bit of foreplay, then she got on top before sliding beneath him. He had never seen a woman cum that quickly, and after, Stan actually felt disappointed by how quick it had been. There was nothing cuddly or romantic about Melanie.

"Do you want a ride home?"

Melanie shook her head. "Nope. I'll take a taxi." Melanie waved and walked out the door. "See you in the park."

That first date pretty well summed up Stan's short relationship with Melanie: a quick tour of a park or a botanical garden, then an expensive meal, which Melanie paid for in cash. Then, they went to his place and had sex.

They got on reasonably well, but Stan found her shallow and boring. All she ever talked about was things. All she ever read was fashion mags.

During their few months together, Stan learned little about her. She never spoke of her past or much about her present. They always went to his place, so he never saw the inside of her house.

One evening Melanie was in bed with her arms crossed over his breasts. She seemed cold and pensive.

"You know what I like about you?" she said.

"What's that?'

"You don't hassle me with a lot of nosy questions. I mean, most guys would pester me about my husband, and who I am and where I go, and all that, but you never do. I like that."

"Glad to hear it."

Melanie reached out and grabbed a handful of Stan's hair. "I want to fuck."

*

That November, the weather was cold, and the mornings foggy, and it wasn't pleasant working in the park. When he arrived, Stan spent as much time as he could in the heated tool shed doing paperwork before he went out mulching. He wore a coat and tuque, thick gloves and a heavy cotton shirt but found that his feet kept getting cold. Still, Stan was no slacker and always put in a good day's work.

Despite his own discomfort, Stan felt especially sorry for Fred and Agnes, who spent their days shivering. They huddled in cheap sleeping bags at night by the creek under a makeshift tent, trying to stay warm by drinking white rotgut. During the day, they lurched about looking for empty bottles and shouting for no apparent reason, and Stan only wished they would go to a warm homeless shelter, but they didn't, preferring the park's isolation.

Several days had passed without a trace of Melanie, and he was starting to think she wouldn't come back, which was all right because, for him, it was now more routine than pleasure.

But one drizzly afternoon, he was mulching a flower bed when he felt a playful hand pinch him.

Stan whirled round and saw a smirking Melanie standing behind him. "How ya doin'?" Her voice was higher than usual. Again, she pinched him.

Stan managed a smile. "You took me by surprise."

"You were daydreaming."

"As usual," he replied.

"So, you still talking to me?" Melanie had wanted to rent a luxury car on their last date, an idea Stan had loudly rejected.

Stan shrugged. "Yeah, I guess."

"Glad to hear it." Melanie leaned forward and kissed him. "You want to get together?"

"Yeah, I guess," he answered slowly. Stan always had a hard time turning people down.

"Good." Now her tone was abrupt and final, as if she had just closed a deal like buying a car or selling a house.

"But maybe we could do something different," he suggested. "I mean, we've pretty well seen every botanical garden there is." He hesitated. "So how 'bout a movie, or maybe we could go bowling or play pool or something?"

Stan could tell that Melanie wasn't into plebeian activities like pool or bowling. She much preferred esoteric things like a botanical garden, then a fashionable restaurant where she could be seen drinking champagne and eating expensive food. However, Stan spent all day working outside in the cold and wanted some place lively and warm.

"What about an art gallery?" he proposed.

"Yeah, that might be okay."

"Great," said Stan with a relieved smile. "I know just the place."

Melanie nodded. "Sounds good," but then Stan noticed she wasn't paying attention, instead peering at something or someone in the distance. Stan glanced over his shoulder and saw Fred and Agnes shivering between two plane trees, guzzling rotgut, and clapping their hands together for warmth. He looked back at Melanie. She had the troubled expression of a little girl reliving a sad and eerie dream.

*

Stan took Melanie to an alternative art gallery in a grubby part of Vancouver's east side, and from the outset, it was obvious she didn't like it. The art was weird and blatantly gay, in-your-face paintings of butch queers steeling for a fight. The other people were fringe types, leather punks in black jeans and leotards who went outside to smoke Gitanes or reefers. They talked a crude, hip jargon that clearly put Melanie off.

Melanie's fashionable clothes didn't fit the venue either. She was starting to draw curious glances and even sneers.

"Let's go," she whispered. "I've had enough."

"Okay," agreed Stan, but he wanted to stay longer.

He left the gallery feeling guilty and annoyed, guilty because he had taken Melanie to a place she hadn't liked and annoyed because he felt guilty. Again, he wished Melanie would just disappear and let him spend his free time as he wanted.

It was already dark, and the Vancouver street lights lit the road back to suburbia. A steady rain was falling. Stan wasn't in the mood for talking, and the drive was silent and tense, but eventually, Melanie broke the ice.

"Do you know somewhere quiet where we could park?"

Stan didn't know what to think. Did she actually want a heart-to-heart talk? He turned off Grandview Highway and headed down a side street before stopping on a quiet crescent. Nearby, family dogs barked, and in the houses, TV screens flashed. The rain was relentless.

"So, what's happening?" asked Stan.

Melanie didn't say anything. Instead, she unbuckled her seatbelt and leaned toward him.

19

Her right arm reached out and touched the top of his coat, and she began to unzip it. Melanie's fingers lifted his shirt and began to rub his belly, then moved down to his trousers, which she unbuttoned. She lowered her head.
Melanie was brilliant.

*

December came, and Stan was more than fed up with the weather. Every day began with a light drizzle that changed to pouring rain, and booking a last-minute ticket to Belize or Mexico became more and more tempting. He even thought of inviting Melanie, but he hadn't seen her for ten days, and of course, he couldn't phone as he didn't know her number. She always just popped by and suggested they get together. Probably she was with her husband.

*

In the park, there were a few rats. Usually, they lived down by the creek, feeding on garbage left by Fred and Agnes or other rare visitors, but in winter, the cold got to them, and one or two made it into the tool shed.
To deal with them, Stan laid baited traps and poison. He felt on edge, expecting to hear them gnawing or see them darting across the floor. He

knew it was more psychological than real, but he just couldn't stand rats.

A week before Christmas, there was a cold snap, and the temperature hit -12, unusually low for Vancouver. It was so cold that Stan scarcely pretended to work, killing time with inventory, and planning next year's plantings.

Now and then, he went out to check on Fred and Agnes, who, on the third frigid day, disappeared, hopefully to someplace warm.

There was still no sign of Melanie, and in a way, he was starting to miss her.

Because of the bad weather, Stan's work day quickly turned into a long coffee break, and he only hoped some asshole from management didn't show up and start bothering him with stupid questions like why he wasn't outside pruning or whatever. But nobody came by, and Stan took to reading crime novels and listening to music, and late one morning, he was indulging in P.D. James and Pil when he saw a brown flash along the far wall and realized he had just seen a rat.

Instantly he had a sharp adrenalin rush, then quietly got to his feet, his eyes glued to the rodent who was scurrying, stopping, nibbling on the floor. Stan kept his eyes on the filthy creature and silently grabbed a pitchfork. The hunt was on.

He raised the pitchfork and took aim, but the rat either sensed trouble or had seen the pitchfork's prongs flash. It suddenly skittered towards the tool shed door, and Stan went to plan b. Rather than killing it inside, he would try to force it outdoors and kill it there.

Stan stepped forward and, with the pitchfork prongs, flicked the inner door latch. Because of the wind, it banged open, startling the rat who, fearing a trap, tried to retreat, but Stan adroitly blocked its path, so it had to run outside.

The rat rushed across the frozen lawn toward the creek, and Stan, pitchfork raised, went after it, hoping for a final deadly shot.

It was, of course, not an even race. Within seconds Stan had caught up and was about to stab it when it started zigzagging, making it hard to hit. Stan persisted but now knew that he had little chance of killing it. The creek area offered brush cover and trees it could climb.   The rat scurried forward, leapt on a fallen tree, and it was then Stan hurled the pitchfork. It missed by almost a metre before clanging off the tree trunk and landing under a large cedar log.

No one else was around. In the distance, Stan could hear a chainsaw whine.

Stan was wearing a heavy shirt and thick trousers, but no gloves, no tuque. The cold was starting to bother him. His hands numb, he went to retrieve the pitchfork. He stooped down, and with one hand, tried to yank it out, but it was stuck in something, and Stan had to use two hands to free it. He gave a strong tug.

"What the fuck???" he muttered.

Hanging from the pitchfork was a bag, but no ordinary bag. It was not some cheap supermarket thing, but high-tech waterproof with a handle and a zip lock. Moreover, the bag was camouflage green and had been lying under dead leaves. Stan shook his head, wondering what to make of it.

He set the waterproof bag aside, squatted back down, and peered under the log, scraping the leaves away and there he discovered three more bags. Even though it was cold, his hands grew sweaty; his heart pumped hard.

Of course, Stan had heard stories (some of them true) about gardeners finding drugs in their parks, and Stan figured he had stumbled on a dealer's stash. Very likely, the bags contained coke or heroin, which meant he would probably just leave them there or perhaps phone the police. Selling the stuff would be complicated and dangerous, plus he wasn't into peddling hard drugs. If it was weed, that would be a different story.

Stan decided to take one of the bags to the tool shed and have a look inside. His hands were shaky, but his mind was clear.

Cautiously he regained the tool shed and locked the door. He undid the zip lock and pulled the bag open. Inside was another bag. Also, opaque and green. Stan extracted the second bag, which was sealed shut with five plastic clothespins. Controlling his tension, he squeezed the clothespins open and laid them on the bench where he sat. He then took a deep breath and opened the second bag, expecting to see white powder.

But there was no white powder. Just money. Lots and lots of money.

*

Stan spent a nervous afternoon. He was tempted to leave work early but forced himself to stay because the last thing he wanted was to attract attention. He returned to the creek and took the remaining three bags to the tool shed, so he could later move the money somewhere else to count and hide it.

When three-thirty finally came, Stan peeked outside to ensure that nobody was around and then placed the bags in the backseat of his pickup under a blanket. He began to drive, carefully navigating the early rush hour traffic at a steady fifty kilometres an hour. He stopped at an office supplies shop to buy a battery-powered bill counter, then proceeded to his destination.

Stan chose a desolate place to hide the money: a derelict baseball diamond that the municipality had mothballed years ago, leaving only weeds and a closed refreshment stand. Everywhere was strewn garbage.

Stan parked his vehicle behind a clump of trees and went to an old paint can lying beside the home plate. He picked up the can and then banged it on the ground. The lid came off. Stan then fished inside and found the key to the refreshment stand, a secret only a handful of parks staff knew.

He went to the refreshment stand and unlocked the door, then gave it a sharp kick, after which it reluctantly opened. Stan returned to his pickup to fetch a big flashlight, the bill counter, and the four bags of money.

Inside the refreshment stand, it was cold and dark and smelled of hamburger grease and stale beer. But there was a clean table and two chairs, and the flashlight provided more than enough light to count the money. Stan set one of the bags on the table and unzipped it. He then pulled the inner bag out. He placed a wad of bills on the counter and listened as the money shuffled through it.

The first bag contained two hundred and fifty thousand U.S. dollars, and when Stan saw the final total, he smiled and laughed with delight. The euphoria of being rich was starting to take hold, his fear to fade.

Counting the money took several hours. Some of it was in British Pounds, Euros, Swiss Francs, and Canadian dollars. The final tally came to one million three hundred and seventy-two thousand Canadian dollars, and Stan figured he was set for life.

Stan stood up, stretched, and stepped outside. It was now after midnight. The clear sky had gone cloudy, and a warm southern wind was blowing, so the cold snap was finally over. He quietly locked the door behind him and began to walk around, looking for the perfect place to stash his loot.

Behind the refreshment stand, Stan saw a shallow gully with a cement culvert. He walked to the spot but decided against it because the culvert could flood, and there wasn't enough plant cover. The area around his pickup was almost barren, but not far away were a handful of tall cedars, their pungent boughs drooping to the ground. Stan bent down and took a good look. The base of the trees was a perfect hiding place. There were a lot of dead leaves and other rubbish to conceal the money.

Stan hid the bags under separate trees. He then threw some garbage in front of each tree and drew a map of the area.

*

By the time Stan got home, it was two in the morning, and there was little point in going to bed as he probably couldn't sleep. Instead, he sat in his usual armchair, extending his legs and reflecting on what to do next. He decided to sit on the money for six months and not vary his routine in the slightest. In fact, he wouldn't even go back to the hiding place because the owner of the money might start watching him. Anything was possible.

He could buy a condo in Vancouver with the money and then invest the rest, but it would also be risky. In Canada, they would want to know where he had got over a million bucks in cash. It would be smarter to smuggle some of the money out and buy property in Central America. There they wouldn't bother him with awkward questions. Maybe Belize or Honduras. Stan started to imagine his dream home by the sea, and the next thing he heard was the alarm in the bedroom. It was 6:30.

"Jesus," he grumbled. "I dozed off. I shouldn't let my guard down like that."

He rose and stumbled into the bathroom, where he washed. In the kitchen, he devoured some porridge and toast.

Before leaving for work, he gave himself a short talk in the bathroom mirror.

"Just take it easy. Remember: this is just another day. Nothing has changed. Take it cool." He smiled at himself. "Everything will be all right."

When he arrived at work, Fred and Agnes had returned and were on a bench gulping cheap whisky. They looked even more tired and unkempt than usual. Both were somewhere in their sixties but seemed much older. Stan was tempted to go over and chat but thought better of it. It was no time for chatting.

*

Three days passed without incident, and Stan began to feel that, at least for now, he was in the clear. Maybe the money had been stashed for the long term, and the owner would only come back months later.

There was still no sign of Melanie.

*

Stan's parents were divorced. On Christmas day, he had lunch with his dad and later went to his mum's place for supper. His little brother, whom he seldom saw, was there. Stan spent Boxing Day with various relatives.

On New Year's, he went drinking with some gardener buddies and had a nice time. But not once did he mention the money or even hint he was on to something big. Unlike a lot of people, Stan could keep his mouth shut.

He did, however, say that he was dating an older woman named Melanie, adding that she was married. There were a few chuckles and lewd comments.

*

He returned to work on January 2nd, praying that everything would be okay, but he had scarcely driven through the park gate when Agnes stumbled toward him, her expression bleary and troubled, her breath reeking of cheap wine and pear cider. Her reddish-grey hair was a mess, her clothes dirty and rumpled.

"Stan," she croaked. "Stan."

Stan rolled down the window of his pickup. "Agnes. What's happening?"

She reached through the window and clutched at his left arm. "Fred's disappeared."

At first, Stan didn't say anything, then heaved a deep sigh. "When did he first go missing?"

"Yesterday."

"Did anything strange happen?"

Agnes continued to clutch at his arm. "He went into the woods for a crap and didn't come back."

Stan nodded and nervously stroked his chin, convinced Fred's disappearance was connected to the money. Stan hadn't counted on collateral damage. "Have you tried to find him?" he asked.

"I went to the creek and shouted, but there was no answer. Now I don't know what to do."

Agnes's voice broke, and she started to cry, something Stan had never seen her do before. He gently opened the pickup's door and stepped outside. He hugged her.

"Fred will probably turn up. Don't worry. It'll be okay, but I'll take a walk through the woods and see if he's there."

"Maybe we should call the police," she sobbed. Stan didn't reply.

*

Stan commenced his search at the north end of the bush, sweeping east to west, west to east, crossing the creek at least a dozen times. Branches snapped in his face, his shoes skidded on slippery moss, and a couple of deer bolted when they saw him. It was dark, wet, and scary. He felt he was being watched, but probably it was just paranoia.

The search took a long time, but he didn't find Fred.   He told Agnes not to worry, that Fred had probably gone to detox, or been taken in by a friendly neighbour, or got lost, whatever, but Stan didn't believe a word of it.

*

That day quitting time couldn't have come soon enough, and at three-thirty sharp, Stan jumped in his pickup and sped out, leaving a forlorn Agnes to her sorrow. He wasn't sure where to go or what to do, but home was the last place he wanted to be. He needed somewhere crowded and warm and ended up in a lively pub with hot waitresses and a big screen TV. He ordered a burger and fries, bottled beer, and apple pie for dessert.

There was a Canucks game on TV.   Stan started to get into it, even talking hockey with some of the other patrons and shouting when the Canucks scored. But it got late, and Stan knew he'd better leave. He went out to the parking lot, got in his pickup and headed home, all the time paranoid about being followed.

He left the pickup in the underground parkade and took the elevator to his third-floor apartment. He was looking forward to a glass of whiskey and a good night's sleep, but the door was open when he arrived. The lower lock had been removed, and the bolt sawed in two—a professional job.

He entered and saw that the place had been torn apart. In the kitchen, the fridge was pulled out and leaning against the wall. The cupboards and drawers were all open, as was the dishwasher. They had emptied the garbage on the floor. They had even ripped open cereal packages. In the living room, his books were lying everywhere, and the back of the TV had been taken off. The sofa was upside down and the cushions cut to tatters.

He saw that the mattress had been sliced open and the closet and drawers emptied in the bedroom. Thousand of dollars in damage, but as far he could tell, nothing had been stolen. He shook his head in disgust and shuddered from fear.

Upstairs he could hear his neighbours' TV. They were watching the Simpsons. Marge was berating Homer, but Stan couldn't quite make out what they were saying.

"Hello there," a voice said.

Stan whirled in his tracks.

"Surprised to see me?"

"Melanie? What are you doing here?"

Melanie was standing at the bedroom door. Her skin was tanned, and her hair had lightened, so she had obviously been somewhere warm. She was wearing a beige raincoat and holding a glossy gift bag.

"I just thought I'd drop by for a visit. I even brought you a present." She reached into the gift bag and took out a dark object, and held it firmly in her right hand. "Like it?"

Melanie was holding a gun. Her expression was hard, her hand steady. Her eyes had a look he had never seen before, a kind of vicious irritation as if he were an annoying insect. Her voice was dead calm.

"It's a Beretta Subcompact. Semi-automatic. Shoots nine millimetres ammunition. It's great at short range."

"Did you kill Fred?" Stan's voice was a hoarse, trembling croak.

Melanie didn't answer right away, but then she nodded. "I should have killed that useless prick the first time I set eyes on him."

Melanie left the doorway and stepped forward, pointing the Beretta at Stan's chest. "Where's the money?"

The next-door neighbour was running water. In the corridor, a door slammed.

"Melanie," he quavered. "I don't know anything about any money."

Melanie's finger settled on the trigger. "You have ten seconds." She sounded like a growling dog.

When he had to, Stan could think fast, and his mind was now in high gear. Although Melanie had a gun, he realized she was playing a weak hand. He was useless to her dead and too big and strong to overpower and torture. Plus, she didn't know he had found the money, and it would be hard to get away with killing him. They had often been seen together, and he had told a few people about her.

He decided to go for broke. "I don't know anything about any money." He moved toward the bedroom door and started to shout. "Melanie! Don't kill me! Melanie! Don't kill me! Melanie! Don't kill me!"

Upstairs there were footsteps, and the TV went silent.

"Stay still," she growled, but Stan kept coming. When he reached Melanie, he shouldered her aside, then started to run.

"Stan, wait!" he heard her cry. "Stan, please wait!" Her tone was urgent, almost pleading.

But Stan didn't wait. "Melanie! Don't kill me!" he kept shouting.

Stan was next to the kitchen and close to the entrance door. If Melanie was going to kill him, she had to do it now, but he was pretty sure she wouldn't. Still, he ducked low, deked, and dived into the outside corridor. He rolled a bit before jumping to his feet and starting to run.

Swerving, he raced down the corridor and then downstairs to the ground floor, where he banged open a fire door that led to the basement. Now walking fast, he went into the laundry room where a neighbour was doing her washing.

"Good evening," he said with a forced smile.

"Hi there."

Three dryers were humming, and a lone washer was chugging. He looked round, trying to decide his next move. Although the laundry room was in the basement, there were ground-level windows that seemed big enough to crawl through.

Stan took a sorting table and carefully pulled it against the wall. Still smiling at the neighbour woman, he stood on the table and slid open the window,

Stan stood on his tiptoes, extended his arms, and hoisted himself up.

*

Outside it was chilly with a hint of rain in the air. A pale moon was struggling to peek through the clouds, and a light breeze was blowing.

Stan ran for some minutes before stopping in a deserted children's playground, his mind still reeling. Gasping and sweating, he slumped down and tried to relax, which took him several minutes. He then began to think things over.

So, the bread belonged to Melanie. He thought about how she had spent money like water and always paid cash. She had often visited the park, and now he knew why. No doubt her rich husband had been a figment of his imagination, and more than likely, she wasn't even married. Where she had got that much money was a mystery, but it sure as hell couldn't have been legal.

Now what? Stan didn't dare go home, and he certainly didn't want to call the police. If he did that, the money would be gone. What he really needed was a secure place to think.

He checked his watch and saw that it was after midnight. After some thought, he took out his Blackberry and called his father, knowing he would resent a late-night call but would still help him. The phone rang six times before Stan heard the familiar voice, as always soft and wary. "Hello. David Crawford here."

"Hi, dad. It's Stan."

"Hello, Stan. What's up?"

"Dad, I need to ask for a favour."

Dead silence, annoyed anticipation. "Go ahead."

"Well, it's a bit complicated, but when I came home this evening, my apartment was broken into, and the place is a total mess. "

"Have you called the police?"

"Not yet. I'm not sure I will as it looks like they didn't steal anything."

"Really?"

"Yeah. Anyway, I've got a bad feeling about this, and I'm kind of afraid they might come back."

"I see."

"I was wondering if I could crash at your place tonight?"

His father hesitated. "Sure. Okay."

"Thanks. I'll probably come by taxi. I should be there in about forty minutes."

"Okay. Take care."

Stan then dialled Surrey Taxi and gave the dispatcher the address of a nearby house, stressing that he would be waiting outside. When the cab arrived, it was just starting to rain.

When his dad opened the house door, he was wearing a dressing gown. He looked gaunt and tired, which made Stan wonder if his health was okay. Stan reached out and touched him on the arm, which was as affectionate as they ever got.

The two went into the living room. His dad sat on the couch, Stan in an armchair. They cracked a couple of beers, and Stan rehashed the burglary, suggesting there might be a weird vendetta behind it without providing any more details. Thankfully his father didn't ask for any.

They then talked about family, sports, and their jobs, more than an hour passed, and his dad said he'd better go to bed because tomorrow was a working day.

"I understand," said Stan, wishing that he and his father were closer. He watched him leave the room, then lay back on the couch, thinking about Melanie and her Beretta Subcompact.

*

After an almost sleepless night, Stan rose early. He took a taxi home, collected his Toyota pickup, and drove to work. After rolling through the park gate, he grabbed some tools and set to pruning a Manitoba Maple on the park's northeast side. It was the safest place for him because the maple was next to a long crescent lined with houses. The street wasn't busy, but at least some cars went by, so it wouldn't be easy for Melanie to get at him.

He hadn't been working ten minutes when Agnes, her face tormented with worry, approached and began watching him work. Strangely she didn't look drunk.

"Still no sign of Fred?" he asked.

"No. No sign of him." She continued to watch him work. Rain was starting to fall, but it didn't seem to bother her. "I think he's dead."

Stan clipped the end of a maple branch. "Why do you say that?"

"We've been married for over forty years. I know when something's wrong. Fred's dead. I know it."

Stan didn't reply; he just kept on pruning.

"Why won't you call the police?" she demanded as if he had refused to do so. "Do you have something to hide?"

Stan realized that Agnes was a lot more perceptive than he had thought. "All right. I'll call them at coffee break," he promised. "Don't worry. I will."

"I'll believe it when I see it," she sniffed, continuing to watch him work. Stan wished she'd go away.

"So, what happened to the lady who used to come here?"

"What lady?"

"The lady with the nice clothes and hair. I saw her kiss and touch you."

39

"Melanie?"

"I guess."

"I don't know where she is," he snapped. "Now, please go away and let me work."

Coffee time was at ten o'clock, and, true to his word, Stan went into the tool shed and dialled the RCMP. A woman answered, and Stan told her he wished to report a missing person. She asked him a few questions, then transferred him to another extension where he gave the basic facts about Fred and how he had disappeared. The conversation lasted all of ten minutes, and Stan gathered that the RCMP would do little or nothing to find a homeless drunk like Fred Macleod.

He had nonetheless done his duty. What more could Agnes, or anyone else, ask?

*

Stan spent the rest of the morning pruning trees and watching his back, convinced Melanie was spying on him and might try to kill him. After all, she had killed poor old Fred after he had gone into the bush for a crap. He imagined Fred squatting with his trousers down when Melanie emerged, her face hard and cruel. What had she done to him? Had she rubbed broken glass in his eyes or pounded his kidneys while he screamed with pain and terror. And what did she do when it became evident that poor Fred knew nothing about the money? Shoot him and dump his body where it would never be found? And, of course, it had been stupid and unnecessary. Just following Fred for a couple of days would have shown he didn't have the money. Otherwise, he would have been spending it like crazy. Whom did she think she was dealing with - a genius? Stan's emotions went from fear to rage and back again.

The anger helped him pass the time, and before long, it was lunchtime. Stan took his pruners and started to walk back to the tool shed. The sky was bleak, a flock of crows perched on leafless plane trees. Canada geese were pecking the soggy ground.

Not far from the tool shed, Agnes was staring sadly into the wild forest. Again, Stan noticed she wasn't drunk.

Inside the shed, Stan heaved a sigh of relief. Only three and a half hours to go. He had almost made it through the day. He sat on the bench and unpacked his lunch. He took a bite, thinking that the tool shed was a refuge, almost a second home. There was a microwave, a small fridge, and a toilet.

On the wall were his bachelor's degree in horticulture and his other certificates. There were also photos of his parents when they were still married and of his younger brother.

Outside, footsteps squished across the wet grass. There was a sharp knock on the door, but Stan didn't jump up to answer. He winced with annoyance, thinking it had to be Agnes come to nag him about phoning the police. He took a few more bites of his sandwich, then went to see who it was.

But it wasn't Agnes. Instead, Stan found himself face to face with two male RCMP officers. Both were in uniform—big men with moustaches.

"Are you Stan Crawford?" one of them asked.

"That's right."

"A couple of hours ago, you reported a missing person. A guy called Fred Macleod."

"That's right." Never in a million years had Stan expected such a fast response, but the police presence was reassuring.

"Can you show us where Mr. Macleod disappeared?"

Stan nodded. "Actually, his wife would know better than me." Stan looked round and spotted Agnes by the trees he had been pruning. "She's over there. Wait a minute, and I'll go get her."

"Okay."

Stan hurried across the lawn and went to Agnes. "Agnes," he said. "The police have come about Fred. You should come and talk to them."

"Why are they here?" She looked suspicious, her weather-beaten face tight and hostile.

"Because I phoned them, just like I promised. Okay?"

Stan took Agnes by the arm and led her to the police officers. "This is Fred's wife, Agnes.

⚹

The officers decided to have the wilderness area searched. They radioed for help, and ten more officers, assisted by dogs, scoured the entire area but failed to find Fred.

Melanie must have killed him somewhere else.

*

That day after work, Stan consulted a lawyer named Nirmal Singh.

Nirmal Singh's office was located in an ugly strip mall, sandwiched between a fast-food joint and a gay sex shop. In the sex shop's window were large photos of almost nude men. Stan glanced at the pictures, then continued to the lawyer's premises. On the glass door were the words: Singh and Partners, Barristers and Solicitors.   He rang the doorbell.   The door clicked open. Stan entered a large lobby with several doors adjoining the lawyers' offices. In the centre of the room, a pretty young woman with brown skin was sitting at a desk. Standing to her left and right stood two older women, all three looking at a magazine.

Stan waited, expecting one of the women to welcome him, but they ignored him and kept staring at the magazine. The younger woman flipped a page and pointed at a photo.

Stan craned his neck to see what they were looking at and saw a glossy photo of a nude fireman. He made out the words Hot Stuff, Red Hot and Fire. No doubt they had bought the magazine at the gay porn shop next door.

Stan cleared his throat. "Excuse me."

The pretty woman looked up. "What is it?"
"I have a four o'clock appointment with Nirmal Singh."

She frowned and pointed at a door. "He's expecting you."

*

Nirmal Singh's office was almost as big as the lobby.   In the centre was a mahogany desk with family photos on it. On the walls were various law degrees and certificates

Singh was a lithe, dapper man of about fifty. He had a bushy Sikh beard and was sporting a black turban.

"You must be Stan," he said. He stepped forward and extended his hand. "Please sit down."

"Thank you." Stan took a chair near the desk. Singh sat and joined his hands together.

"So, you found a large sum of money?"

"That's right. There's a wildness area near the park where I work, and I went in there and stumbled on it."

The lawyer asked for all the details, so Stan obliged, mentioning Fred, and only omitted where he had hidden the money.

Nirmal Singh smiled. "Interesting story. My job would be a lot more exciting if I had clients like you every day."

Stan smiled back. "So, what should I do?"

"Before you came, I took an hour to go over the laws and precedents for people who find large sums of money. I'm also familiar with a few high-profile cases of this kind."

"Good."

"As far as I can see, you're in a pretty good position. In fact, if you play your cards right, you

45

stand an excellent chance of keeping the money."

"Really?"

"That's right. Your best bet is to turn the money into the local RCMP and, if after a year, nobody comes forward to claim the money, it will be yours."

"What about Melanie?"

Singh nodded. "The woman is very likely a drug dealer or at least a criminal of some kind, so it is highly doubtful that she'll try to claim the money."

"Probably not, but should I tell the police about her?"

Nirmal Singh shook his head. "Do not, under any circumstances, tell the police about her. If you do that, this could become a criminal matter, and you'll end up kissing the money goodbye."

"So, don't tell them about Melanie?"

"Absolutely not. Just keep it simple. You were chasing a rat, threw a pitchfork, and stabbed a bag of money. Then you found three more bags. After that, you hid the money, then thought better of it and decided to turn it in. It might be a good idea to omit the part about hiding the money, but that's up to you. You could even add that you consulted a lawyer."

"But what if she comes back?"

Singh made a clicking noise. "If I were you, I'd lie low for a few days, give yourself time to turn the money in and settle matters with the police. If this Melanie woman has any brains at all, she'll find out that you've gone to the police, especially if she's connected to a criminal gang. Once the police have the money, there's nothing she can do about it. Killing you won't change that."

"No, it won't," agreed Stan.

"If I were you, I wouldn't go home either. Instead, you should stay at a motel and not go to work for a few days. Just phone in sick."

"I could do that. "

Nirmal Singh half-closed his eyes. "My brother-in-law owns a motel on King George Highway. Reasonable rates. If you want, I can give him a call, and he'll send someone to get you. "

Stan hesitated a bit. "Okay. Yeah sure. Give him a call."

"And leave your vehicle in our parking lot. It'll be safe there. You can exit   by the back entrance." "Good, but what about Fred?"

Again, Nirmal Singh shook his head. "Don't mention him either."

"But she killed him. She told me she did."
Singh sighed. "Stan, she might have been bluffing. For all, you know that old lush could

have fallen in the creek or still be alive and kicking, so don't complicate matters by telling the RCMP about him. Just keep it simple."

"All right. But what if the police connect Fred's disappearance with the money?"

Nirmal Singh grinned. "The RCMP are very busy and not all that bright. Stan, it will take them months to connect the two cases, if they ever do at all."

"Glad to hear it."

"Oh, and you can pay before you leave. I'll call my brother-in-law about the motel room. They'll send someone to pick you up."

*

In the outer office, the three women were still staring at nude firemen photos.

"I'd like to pay my bill."

It was the young woman who spoke. "Seventy-five dollars."

"Okay." Stan took out his chequebook. "There you go."

She studied the cheque. "Do you have any ID?"

Stan produced his driver's licence, and she wrote down the details and made a photocopy. She gave back his licence, and Stan took a chair in the reception area. The three women returned to their porn mag.

*

Nirmal Singh's brother-in-law arrived promptly and drove Stan to a modest motel not far from the Fraser River. Stan checked in and was taken to a room located at the back of the building with a parking lot for a view.

The room was simple: a single bed, a bedside table, two cheap chairs, and a TV. Thankfully, in the bathroom, there were toiletries as he had come unprepared.

Stan was still unnerved by the day's events. He tried watching TV but couldn't focus. He began to pace up and down and decided to dial room service for a six-pack of beer. Again, the service was prompt.

Stan took the six-pack and flopped on the bed. He opened a bottle and took a long swig, some of it dribbling on his chin which he wiped with the bed sheet. The beer began to take hold, and he managed a weary smile. He had downed the first beer in less than two minutes and right away opened a second, which he drank more slowly.

"Jesus Christ," he murmured. "What a fucking day."

He pictured Melanie and her Beretta semi-automatic and the weird look in her eyes. Again, he wondered how he hadn't realized that the money belonged to her.

Stan opened a third beer and yawned, thinking of Agnes and how grief-stricken she was over Fred. Sadly, it was ironic that a dirt-poor drunk like Agnes had someone to love while he was all alone.

Fatigue and alcohol soon meant Stan dozed off, but nightmares of rats' money and Melanie tormented his sleep. Fred was screaming for mercy as Melanie tortured him and a heartbroken Agnes weeping for her beloved husband as Stan, guilt-ridden and powerless, looked on. Once or twice he tried to intervene but became paralyzed.

About three a.m., he jerked awake, covered in sweat, his stomach queasy from beer. For several minutes he lay there, trying to calm his anxiety, then got to his feet and went to the window. He pulled back the curtain and viewed a dull grey parking lot lit by a solitary lamp post. Everything was dead quiet.

He then did some yoga postures, which cleared his mind and helped him relax

*

Stan parked his rented Buick Skylark on a hill, then took his binoculars and got out. He walked behind the car and began to scan the area where he had hidden the money. He moved the binoculars from left to right, looking for people but saw no one, only birds, squirrels, weeds and strewn garbage. Under a tree, a coyote was chewing on a dead pigeon.

He turned and viewed the potholed road leading to the baseball diamond to determine if he had been followed. Stan suspected he had been too quick to accept staying at that motel as it could have been a set-up. He was apprehensive that Nirmal Singh or his brother-in-law might have trailed him from the motel hoping to steal the money.

His eyes moved down and beside the road, scanning the edges for human life, but again there was none. The money was making him paranoid.

Stan drove the Skylark down to the baseball diamond and parked the vehicle next to the abandoned refreshment stand. Without closing the door, he stepped out and strode toward the hiding place.

In nearby trees, crows were standing guard, and under them, the coyote was watching him. When Stan got closer, it bared its teeth. Stan just kept walking.

The garbage he had put in front of the spruce trees was still there. He bent down, yanked away the debris, then fished out the first of the four bags. It was slick and wet, as were the other three.

His arms full, Stan took the bags to the car, set them on the ground, opened the trunk and placed the bags inside. Then, he got in the car and drove away.

*

"So, tell me about the money."

Stan was in a small office in the north wing of RCMP -Surrey headquarters. Sitting across from him was police Lieutenant Debra Spilchuk, a stocky woman of about forty with dark hair and frank blue eyes. She was wearing civilian clothes.

He leaned forward in his chair and clasped his hands. "I'm not sure where to begin."

"Try the beginning."

"Okay. One day I was at work and found a large sum of money."

"As simple as that?" Spilchuk was sitting back with her hands on her lap.

Stan told her about the cold weather and how a rat had got into the tool shed and how he had chased it with his pitchfork and ended up stabbing a bag full of money.

Lieutenant Spilchuk pointed to the bag in question. "So that's why it has holes in it?"

"That's right. I scored a direct hit."

"Then what?"

"I took one of the bags into the shed and opened it. I figured it would be cocaine or heroin, but it was money. So I counted the money and decided to turn it in."

"Good idea. Have you consulted a lawyer?"

"Yeah, I have."

"What's his name?"

"A guy called Nirmal Singh."

Spilchuk frowned. "That prick. So, no doubt you know the rules about finding money. If it goes unclaimed for a year, then it's yours. "

"That's what Mr. Singh told me."

"He also probably told you to shut up about certain details, like whether you initially hid the money and who the owner of the money might be and stuff like that, right?"

Stan blushed and shrugged. "He's a good lawyer."

Spilchuk didn't insist. "You'll have to sign several documents, and a notary will have to witness your signature. Plus, the money will be officially counted here in RCMP headquarters and then put away for safe keeping. Can you come back tomorrow?"

"Yeah, I guess."

"Good. Be here at eleven tomorrow morning."

Stan got to his feet. "See you tomorrow."

*

That year spring came early. A warm wind bathed the Vancouver area, and by mid - February, the crocuses and cherry trees were in bloom. It was a busy time for a gardener, and Stan spent his days spreading manure and preparing flower beds for planting.
Every day a crew of seasonal workers came to help.

When May arrived, Stan and the crew spent their days bent down, holding trowels, planting marigolds, salvia, and alyssum. It was hard on the back, and quitting time never came too early. After work, Stan often enjoyed a beer with the crew.

Melanie and the money began to fade into the background. He was almost happy.

But there was still one thing that gnawed at him, and that was Fred and Agnes. Fred had now been gone for almost five months and, even though he knew it was stupid, Stan still blamed himself for Fred's death. Above all, he felt guilty for not telling the police about Melanie and how he suspected - knew - that she had killed Fred.

Agnes was still in the park but, mentally, she was going downhill fast. She spent her days wandering about drunk, often going into the wild space, and when Stan saw her, she was always muttering to herself or having an imaginary conversation with Fred. Sometimes she started crying, "Fred! Fred! Fred!" He tried talking to her, but it was little use.

Somehow, she managed to scrounge enough food to survive, but Stan doubted if she'd make it through another winter.

So far, nobody had phoned mental health about her, but it was only a matter of time. Unless salvation came, Agnes was destined to end her days in a mental institution. Stan felt even the park was better than that.

But, on a sparkling June morning, salvation did come. Stan had got up in a good mood, had a healthy breakfast, and promptly gone to work. When he drove through the park gate, he noticed Agnes talking to an old gent near the tool shed and wondered who it could be. It wasn't until he was almost on top of them that he recognized him, and even then, he looked three times to be sure.

Stan braked hard and flew from his pickup. With a huge grin, he rushed forward and grabbed his shoulders.

"Fred! Jesus Christ! I can hardly believe it." He shook Fred's shoulders. "Where the hell have you been, buddy? We thought you were dead."

Fred blushed and beamed, and Stan again shook his shoulders. He had never been so happy to see anyone. He looked Fred up and down and smiled.

"Jesus Christ, buddy. You're lookin' good!"

It was true. Fred was well-groomed and clean-shaven. His eyes were clear, and it was as if he had lost ten years during a five-month absence.

"Where the hell have you been?"

"Stan, what happened is this:"

Fred unfolded a tale of kindness and redemption. After going into the wild space for a crap, he had headed north to go garbage-picking, rummaging for New Year's bottles in people's back yards. He wasn't disappointed, finding more than forty bottles, which he stored in a large gunny sack, and everything was fine until he started to feel dizzy and sick. He sat on a garbage can, then fainted and fell to the ground. He lay there until someone found him.

"Her name was Martha Sutton," explained Fred.

Martha Sutton was an Anglican vicar. She spotted Fred and called her husband, and together they took Fred to the emergency. Fred spent three days in Surrey Memorial Hospital before being released.

"Didn't the police find you?"

"Yeah, they did. The cops phoned to see if a guy with my name had been admitted. Then one of them came to talk to me, and I told them I was okay and not to worry."

"And then what?"

"Well, then Martha took me under her wing." Fred had been taken to a rehabilitation centre and, incredibly, managed to stop drinking. The first week was complete hell, but with Martha Sutton's kind guidance, Fred hung on and was now completely sober.

"I haven't had a drink in five months," he said, standing like a proud soldier.

Stan grinned and slapped him on the back. "Way to go, buddy. I'm proud of you. I'd never thought I'd see the day."

"Right now, I've got my own room, and I'm collecting my old age pension."

Stan imagined the modest circumstances, but it was still a hell of a lot better than the park.

"But why didn't you come to visit or at least call?" he asked. "I mean, poor Agnes was half crazy. And I was worried too. I figured someone had killed you."

"Stan, I was afraid to."

"Afraid?"

"I was afraid that if I did that, I'd start drinking again. I just wasn't strong enough. It's not until recently that I've felt strong enough to visit."

Fred sounded like a bad actor rehearsing his lines, and Stan could tell he was lying. Likely Fred had decided to dump Agnes and then had a change of heart.

"Right now, I'm trying to convince Agnes to leave the park, but she just doesn't want to." Stan, who had scarcely looked at Agnes, now turned his attention to her. She seemed tired and wretched but less confused as if she had regained her bearings.

"I don't want to leave the park," she declared. Fred shook his head with exasperation. "I just don't understand this. I hate the park."

"So, do I," Stan heard himself say.

"I don't want to leave the park," Agnes repeated.

*

August came. Stan and the crew had finished planting late-summer annuals, forget-me-nots and wallflower- and were now placing protective netting and fences so squirrels and crows wouldn't eat them. It was tough, finicky work that made his back sore.

But despite his sore back, Stan was feeling good about life. The money was safe, and in only five months, it would be his. Fred returned from the dead, which had lifted an enormous burden from his mind, and Melanie had disappeared. Agnes remained in the park, but knowing Fred was alive meant her condition had improved, and she wasn't drinking nearly as much. In addition, she looked better than before. Two or three times a week, Fred came to the park and tried to talk her into leaving, but she stubbornly refused, something Fred and Stan simply didn't understand. Still, Stan figured it was only a matter of time until Agnes gave in and left.

But there was another reason for Stan's happiness, and her name was Flavia. He had met her two months ago at UBC botanical gardens where Flavia was in charge of the rhododendron section. Finding her attractive, Stan had strolled over and commenced asking questions about rhododendrons. Later they went for coffee, and it had continued from there.

They now saw each other at least three times a week, going to alternative films, parks, gardens, restaurants. During the week, they slept at Flavia's west-side place, but every Saturday, she cycled to Surrey and met Stan in the park. After they had lunch, they went on a nature walk.

Her last name was Carlotta, her parents, Italian immigrants from Milan. She was tall and sinewy with black curly hair. She was thirty-one. Like Stan, she had never been married and had never lived with anyone.

They had only been dating a few months, but Stan already felt she was the love of his life. He told Flavia about his plans: quitting his job and buying a condo. He told her he'd make sure the condo was big enough for two. When he said that, she smiled and kissed him.

*

Summer turned to fall and fall to winter. The time had gone quickly, and on January 13th, money day arrived. Stan took a day off and, at 10:30 am sharp, arrived at the police station where Lieutenant Spilchuk was waiting for him. As before, she was wearing street clothes. With her were a notary public and a witness.

"Would you like coffee?" asked Spilchuk.

"Sure would."

"Well, we don't have any."

Stan stiffened with surprise, but then Spilchuk smiled, and Stan saw she was joking.

"Martha," she said to the civilian employee. "Would you mind getting us some coffee?"

"No problem."

"Have a chair," said Spilchuk.

Stan sat down, and the notary public, a woman in her late fifties, explained the procedure for acquiring the money, which entailed signing a load of documents and then requesting that the sum be transferred to his bank account.

The whole thing took forty-five minutes, and when Stan left the RCMP building, he felt wild and free. He was a young millionaire with a good life ahead of him. He'd give his notice at the parks board in another month and get down to seriously looking for a condo in East Vancouver, preferably an Italian neighbourhood where he and Flavia could watch Italian soccer and drink espresso. Good-bye Surrey.

Once the condo was bought, he'd open his own private gardening business and get clients through advertising and word of mouth. He had a few leads.

*

The Saturday morning sun was already high, the temperature cool but pleasant, and Stan was in the park waiting for a sweaty and smiling Flavia to arrive on her mountain bike. He was looking forward to their day together, their first day after the money.

But several minutes had passed, and the usually punctual Flavia was late. Stan got off the tree stump, wandered around a bit, then decided to pay Agnes a quick visit as she wasn't far, camped out by the creek in a makeshift tent made of wood, plastic, and cardboard. Fighting his way through brush and branches, he found the tent but didn't see Agnes. He listed the plastic flap and looked in. She wasn't there.

"Agnes!" he called. "Agnes!' No reply. Just the sound of birds and water rushing.

He prowled around a bit longer but then abandoned the search and returned to the tool shed. By the time he got there, it was almost nine, and Flavia still hadn't arrived. Something was wrong as she always called when she was late.

He took out his Blackberry and tried to call her. No answer. He waited another twenty minutes and called again, but nothing. Stan's active imagination clicked into high gear. Flavia must have been injured in an accident or maybe murdered and raped. He began to pace up and down, but then his Blackberry rang, and the screen showed Flavia's number. Stan smiled and answered.

"Hi, Flavia!"

"Hi, Stan. It's Melanie."

At first, Stan was too dumbfounded to say anything. "Melanie?"

"Surprise, surprise." Her voice was hoarse, almost broken, but it was definitely Melanie.

"How did you get hold of Flavia's phone?"

"Never mind that, Stan. We need to talk about money."

Stan didn't say anything. His palms were moist, his heart racing. Sweat was dripping down his body.

"I take it you'd like to see Flavia again, right?"

"Yes."

"Well, then you'd better do what I tell you because, if you don't, you won't see her again. At least not alive. You understand?"

"Yeah."

"I want all the money by Monday night. Go to the bank, take it out, and leave it where I tell you. Understand?"

"Okay."

Melanie told Stan to leave the money under a fast-food dumpster at 2300 on Monday night.

"Okay. I will."

"I hope so. Don't try to call me again, Stan. The number won't work. Also, don't call the police, because I'm serious about killing her. Bye."

*

Stan returned to the tree stump and tried to think. In just a few short minutes, his whole life had been shattered. A murderess had taken Flavia hostage, and the money might well be gone. He didn't know what to do.

He was so distressed that he didn't hear Agnes approach him.

"Stan, what's the matter?"

Startled, Stan looked up. "Oh, I've just had some terrible news."

Agnes was wearing a heavy rain coat Fred had given her. Her hair was more or less combed, and she seemed sober. "That's too bad, Stan. I'm sorry."

"Thanks."

"Stan, I've got something important to tell you."

"What's that?"

"I saw my daughter, Heather."

"Who?"

"Heather, Stan. I saw Heather, my daughter."

More than thirty years had passed since they had taken Fred and Agnes's kids away.

"Where?"

"Here in the park."

"Here? How could she have been here?"

"You saw her too."

"I saw her?" asked Stan.

Agnes nodded. "The lady with the nice hair and clothes. She was your girlfriend, then she disappeared."

Stan frowned and was about to tell Agnes to go away, but something warned him not to. The story was just too bizarre to be untrue.

"My girlfriend is your daughter? You mean Melanie?"

"Her name is Heather Macleod."

"Okay. Heather Macleod. Agnes, you wouldn't by any chance have a picture of her anywhere?"

"Yes," she said decisively. "In my shopping cart."

"Do you think you could show it to me?"

Agnes turned around then lurched toward the forest. Stan watched her disappear into a thicket and observed the tree branches twitch as she fumbled for what was sure to be an old photo. Of course, there was no guarantee that she'd find it amidst all the junk she toted around, but Stan dearly hoped she would.

As he waited, Stan began to put two and two together. He recalled the first time he had met Melanie and her peculiar curiosity about Fred and Agnes. He remembered touring Queen Elizabeth Gardens and Melanie laughing about the Heather Section and how he had said she must be Scottish, which Melanie had denied. And, despite his own distress, Stan could see more heartbreak coming as Agnes's long-lost daughter was a desperate criminal. Another heartbreak was something Agnes (and Fred) didn't need.

Agnes emerged from the bushes. She was holding a photo.

"Here."

Stan took the photo, a withered old colour snapshot from a cheap camera. He held it up to the light and squinted. The years had taken their toll, but the little girl in the blue dress was definitely Melanie.

He forced a smile. "Agnes, have you stayed in the park all these months waiting for Melanie to come back?"

"Her name's Heather. Heather Macleod."

Stan sighed. "Have you been waiting all this time for her?"

"That's right," she said stiffly. "I was hoping she'd come back."

"I'm sorry, Agnes, but you're mistaken. There is no way the girl in the photo is your Heather. They're two completely different people."

Agnes flushed. "She's our daughter, Heather."

"Agnes, there's no way she's your daughter. I've met her parents, and she looks just like them. Her name's Melanie Horvath. And that's a fact."

Stan could tell she was wavering. All she needed was a little push, and she'd leave the park with Fred.

"She isn't your daughter, Agnes. So, you might as well forget all about her."

"I was sure it was her. I wanted to talk to her and say I was sorry for being such a bad mother."

Stan reached out and took her hand. "It's too late for that. Right now, your best bet is to leave the park and go with Fred."

"You're probably right. It's not very nice here."

"It isn't. But you said you'd seen Melanie. When was that?"

"This morning."

"Here in the park?"

"Yes. She was here. Just before you arrived, then she went away."

"Did she see you?"

Agnes shook her head. "I don't think so."
Agnes placed her hands on her hips, then turned and pointed. "She lives over there."
"How do you know that?"
"Because I watched where she went. She went over there and into one of the houses."
Agnes was pointing at a cul-de-sac.
"Do you know which house?"
"The white one."

*

In the tool shed, Stan used the landline to call the police. A woman's voice answered, and Stan asked to speak to Lieutenant Spilchuk, knowing she was probably off duty.

"What do you want to talk to Lieutenant Spilchuk about?"

"A hostage-taking," he replied. "It's very important.

A minute later, and much to his surprise, Spilchuk was on the line.

"This is Lieutenant Spilchuk."

"Stan Crawford. You remember me?"

"The guy who found the money."

"That's right. I need to talk to you about something important."

"What's that?"

"A hostage-taking."

Stan related the facts as best he could, speaking for about three minutes without interruption.

"Where are you now?" she asked.

"In the park where I work. "Stan explained where it was and how to get there. "I'll be waiting outside the tool shed."

"Okay. Stay put. I'll be there in about ten minutes."

*

When Stan left the tool shed, he saw Fred and Agnes walking hand in hand toward the forest's edge. Right away, he knew something big had happened as it was the first he'd ever seen them holding hands. It was even more telling when Fred entered the bush, then returned with Agnes's cumbersome, filthy shopping cart, which he pushed forcefully toward the park gate while Agnes, perhaps a trifle slowly, followed behind.

Stan did not doubt that they were leaving the park for good. He felt sad because, in a way, he was losing friends. Stan sighed and looked at his watch. It was nearing nine-thirty. The sky was clouding over, the wind picking up.

A white Honda Accord entered the park and stopped in the visitors' section. From it emerged a stocky woman in a dull grey jogging suit. The woman opened the back door and out bounded a golden retriever, which she grabbed by the collar and then put on a leash. Dog and woman commenced running around the park.

Stan watched them run along the far side of the park, then circle right before coming toward the tool shed, where the woman stopped to catch her breath.

"He's too fast for me. I should have brought a bulldog."

"Might have been better," agreed Stan. "Do the RCMP even have bulldogs?"

Spilchuk smiled and shook her head. "No, we don't. The only other choice was a German shepherd."

She patted the dog on the head. "Sit!" The golden retriever obeyed, and the leash slackened.

"So, where's this woman who kidnapped your girlfriend?"

"She might be watching us right now."

"Then don't point. Just tell me where."

"The white house in the cul de sac over there."

Spilchuk discreetly turned to look, then nodded. "Do you know the name of the Cul de Sac?"

"Robert Service."

"Anything else you could tell me?"

Stan mulled it over, deciding not to tell her that Melanie's real name was Heather Macleod and that her parents had lived in the park.

"Nothing that I can think of."

Spilchuk tugged at the dog's leash. "Come on, boy. Let's go."

Spilchuk broke into the run and once again circled the park before regaining the white Honda Accord. She and the dog got back in. The car began to move and briefly entered the Cul de Sac. No doubt Spilchuk would radio the address to RCMP headquarters.

*

Stan went to his pickup and got his binoculars. He entered the forest and climbed a tall birch with early buds. He sat on a comfortable branch offering a perfect view of the Cul de Sac, training his binoculars on the white house where Melanie (Heather) held Flavia hostage.

*

It didn't take long for things to happen. Within ten minutes, three RCMP squad cars drove up and blocked access to the Cul de Sac. Six officers disembarked and crouched behind the vehicles' front doors. Their pistols were drawn, and Stan saw a high-powered scope rifle, obviously meant to kill Melanie if necessary. Stan couldn't see behind the house but knew there had to be more officers in the alley.

Nearby two ambulances were waiting, the crew young and energetic.

Another two squad cars arrived and sealed off the crescent, and then Spilchuk drove up in the Honda Accord. In the backseat were two German Shepherds and beside her, in the passenger seat, was a big man with a moustache. Spilchuk was talking on the phone. With the binoculars, he watched her lips move.

At that point, he wasn't sure how much time had passed, but his buttocks were starting to hurt from sitting on the birch branch, and the cool spring wind was starting to bite through his jacket. He glanced at the sky and saw that clouds were thickening; he hoped it didn't rain.

Suddenly he heard Spilchuk's voice. "Melanie Horvath! Can you hear me? Can you hear me? If you can, we want to talk to you. Please listen to us."

She was using a microphone. "Melanie, we need to talk. If you can, please call the following telephone number. 525-3617."

The white house looked calm and mundane. Typical suburbia. One storey. A driveway. A lawn. There was a big picture window, but the drapes were drawn so that he couldn't see inside. Had Melanie been living there all this time?

"Melanie, don't panic! Talk to us! You have options! Tell us what you want!"

A covey of pigeons swept by, their grey feathers blending with the sky.

"Melanie! Talk to us! Don't panic!"

But then Stan heard semi-automatic gunfire and saw a swarm of police officers rushing the house, running low, their weapons out. They tried the front door, but it didn't open. With a battering ram, they smashed it down.

There were three more shots. Dogs were barking. People were watching from their front lawns.

An ambulance, siren wailing, drove up. The crew jumped out and, carrying a stretcher, hurried inside. Somewhere a cell phone rang.

Stan lifted his binoculars.

From the front door, the ambulance crew emerged with someone on the stretcher. At first, Stan couldn't get a clear view as the medics were in the way, and it wasn't until the stretcher was placed in the vehicle that he caught a glimpse of the wounded person. She was wearing an oxygen mask, but there was a flash of blond hair and fair skin: Melanie.

The ambulance departed.

Another ambulance arrived, but this time the crew moved more slowly as if there was no emergency. They didn't even take a stretcher, and Stan now knew Flavia was dead.

On the ground below, a family of skunks sauntered by.

Clenching the binoculars, Stan saw a red-coated ambulance attendant leave the house. She was smiling, and behind her was a young woman with black curly hair. Pale and shaken, but walking strong. Flavia was alive.

Stan jumped down and began to run.

Paris and Marie

"Okay, Gilles. You've got the job."

Gilles Leclerc was sitting in the main office of an exclusive Parisian racquets club called Élan. On the far wall was a French flag, and elsewhere photos of champion tennis, squash, and badminton players who had trained at Élan. There was also a large glass case with trophies Élan teams had won.

With Gilles were two women: Monique Guérin and Céline de Vasseur.

"Thank you very much, Monique," said Gilles. "I'm glad to be part of the Élan team."

"I'm sure you'll be a great asset," replied Monique Guérin with a friendly smile. She was a tall, athletic woman in her forties. She was also Gilles' personal squash coach.

"So am I," interjected Céline de Vasseur, who was sitting next to Monique. Céline was petite and fashionable and worked for a multinational called Dynamic Finance in the HR department.

Behind the two women, through the office window, Gilles could see people playing tennis in the brilliant Parisian sunshine, green balls smashing the red clay surface.

"Well, I suppose we should do the paperwork," said Monique Guérin. From her desk, she took a folder and handed it to Gilles. "Are you ready to sign?"

"I believe so, but I'll take one last look before I do." Gilles was wearing shorts and a Tee-shirt. On the floor was his equipment bag.

Gilles scanned the document to ensure that no unexpected, last-minute changes had been made, but everything was in order: Gilles Leclerc, budding squash star, would provide coaching services at Élan Racquets Club and be expected to play a series of exhibition matches. In exchange, he would receive three thousand euros a month, a modest flat in Montmartre, plus a range of other benefits and bonuses.

He had already signed a separate agreement with Dynamic Finance, stating he would train some of their forex squash team.

Gilles took out a pen, signed, then handed the document to Monique. "Good to have you aboard," she said, adding: "And I'll see you on Thursday at noon for our training session. That exhibition match is coming up."

Gilles nodded. "Yeah. See you then." He looked over at Céline de Vasseur. "Well, Céline, Monique's a busy woman, so we shouldn't take up any more of her time."

"Quite right," answered Céline de Vasseur, rising from her chair. "Let's go meet the guys."

*

Céline de Vasseur led Gilles down a flight of stairs and by the outdoor tennis courts where players, some famous, were, training hard. Gilles wished he could stop and watch, but there was no time for that.

They left the tennis section and passed a shimmering sapphire pool. White-coated waiters were serving the customers, among them beautiful women in skimpy bikinis, and again Gilles wished he could stop and look.

They returned inside, went down a corridor, and entered the din of the squash section where people were hammering small black balls with their racquets. Each court was occupied.

Here Céline de Vasseur slowed down, giving Gilles a chance to watch. At first glance, it seemed the level of squash at Élan was moderately high. Most of the players were in their thirties or forties, very likely business people. As usual, the majority were men, but there were four women players, one of whom Gilles thought he recognized.

"Is that Marie Sinclair?"

"That's right," said Céline de Vasseur. She stopped walking. "Marie's an ardent squash player."

Marie Sinclair was a prominent journalist who often read the TV news. Tall and slender, she had gorgeous black hair and an exotic, vaguely Asian face. She moved with grace and aggression on the squash court, smashing the ball deep, dominating the centre, keeping her opponent off stride. Finally, she hit a game-winner and punched the air.

Céline smiled and waved. Marie Sinclair grinned back.

"You know her?" asked Gilles.

"Yeah. We're actually friends. Marie's does some consulting work for Dynamic Finance. That's where I met her."

"Small world," remarked Gilles.

They continued, climbing a staircase that led to a bar called The Last Serve to meet the forex squash team, but before entering, Céline paused and squeezed his arm.

"Gilles, before introducing you, I think there is something I should say."

"What's that?"

"As you know, Dynamic Finance has spent a certain amount of money on our squash programme. For us, it's a key part of our team-building process for forex traders and executives."

"Of course."

"Well, it's important that the guys take it seriously. "She was standing close, looking him straight in the eye. "Whatever you do, don't let them slack off. Make sure they train hard and, above all, don't take any bullshit. Understand?"

"I understand," said Gilles.

"If there's any problem, just let me know."

"I will." She released his arm.

In the bar, the men were sitting down, all five wearing shorts and Tee-Shirts. Their equipment bags were nearby.

"Bonjour," said Céline. "It's good to see you're all here."

"We came early," one said with a smile.

"Gentlemen," said Céline. "This is Gilles Leclerc. He's the new squash coach who will be training you and getting you ready for the tournaments in the corporate squash league."

Gilles nodded and gave a quick smile. He then shook their hands and eyed them like an officer appraising troops. In their late twenties or early thirties, the five men were youngish, financial whiz-kids who had gone to the right schools and risen fast on the corporate ladder.

"Well," said Céline. "I'll leave you to it. I've got to get going."

"Au revoir," they said.

Gilles remained standing. "Well, messieurs, what I've got in mind is for today what you might call a getting acquainted session. I'd like to play a game or so with each of you, make a few notes, and then discuss it with you later up there. It will only take an hour. While I'm playing with one of you, I want the other four to do drills. First boast and drives, then down the wall. Got it?"

One gave a humorous salute. "Yes, sir."

*

The first Gilles played with was Rachid Naziz, a Frenchman of Algerian origin. Twenty-nine, dark curly hair, he was of medium height and had an engaging smile. Gilles, who had already read up on the five men, knew Rachid was a top forex trader.

Rachid didn't seem nervous facing a world-class squash player, actually eager for the challenge.

Gilles put on his safety glasses. "You can serve first."

Rachid, who was left-handed, lob-served from the right of the court. Gilles hammered the ball hard down the left wall, and, to his credit, Rachid raced across and returned, albeit weakly. Gilles then volleyed cross-court, and again

Rachid returned, but it was awkward and rushed. Finally, Gilles drove the ball to the left, moved to the T, and then watched Rachid lunge and try to boast, but it didn't make the front wall.

"1-0," called Gilles.

It didn't take long for Gilles to observe Rachid's strengths and weaknesses and, after winning 11-0, Gilles shook his hand.

"Good work, Rachid."

"Thanks." Rachid was sweating and breathing hard.

"Okay. Go practice with the others."

Gilles left the court, sat down, and wrote what he thought of Rachid's game on a chart. He then rose and went to observe the other men, only to discover that, on one court, a player was talking on his mobile while the other was practising straight drives alone.

Gilles frowned and tapped his racquet on the glass back wall. "Why aren't you practising?"

The man, Pierre Gauthier, looked startled, almost shocked as if being interrupted was surreal. He blushed, scowled, then muttered something into his mobile and rang off.

"Come and play," Gilles barked, and Pierre Gauthier followed him to the available court.

"All right. Let's have a quick game. You can serve."

Still scowling, Pierre Gauthier served the ball high and deep. Gilles returned hard and bolted to the T when, to his surprise, Gauthier faked a drive, then tried a clever drop shot that landed soft and tight to the left wall. This good shot would have fooled most players, but not Gilles, who easily reached it and then played a drop shot. Pierre Gauthier scarcely reacted to the return. 1-0.

They resumed play, and it was soon apparent that Pierre Gauthier was a skilled yet lazy player not in great condition.

After Gilles had won 11-0, he patted Gauthier on the shoulder and told him to start practising. Gilles subsequently played with the other three team members and made quick, careful notes. Then, he led them up to the bar where he ordered a large lemonade and remained standing while the five men, still puffing, flopped down and rested.

Gilles allowed a couple of minutes before delivering his verdict.

"Messieurs," he began. "A lot of work has to be done. There are too many basic mistakes, and some of you need to improve your conditioning. Sometimes a work ethic is also lacking."

"Specifically, Rachid, you have to improve your body mechanics. Too often, you're leaning over to hit the ball and not bending your knees.

You have to keep your back straight and turn square to the wall, but we'll work on that. However, the effort is there."

Rachid nodded, not offended in the least.

"Jacques, you have to improve court movement. You're just not efficient. You waste a lot of energy."

Jacques Bertrand, blond, in his early thirties, nodded and serenely accepted Gilles' opinion.

"As for Georges, you have to learn to be more patient. You have all the shots, but you keep trying for winners that don't score. That won't work against better players, and in the league, there will be some pretty good players. However, I'd say you have talent and can play a lot better. I'd say conditioning might be a problem, and that's why you're trying to end the rallies quickly."

"I agree," said Georges. Georges Lanthier was thin and wiry but a touch too tall for squash. He had dark hair and eyes.

"As for Jean-Luc, you have to stop daydreaming. Something tells me your mind is elsewhere. Maybe on your girlfriend or maybe on the job. Maybe both. Otherwise, I'd say you have talent and can hit the ball well."

Jean-Luc de Beaumais had light blond hair and handsome, jagged features. He blushed and nodded as Gilles had hit the mark. The other men smirked.

"Finally, Pierre, I think there are a few problems you need to work on. Above all, your work ethic. I get the impression you're trying to surf on your talent, and that won't get you anywhere. You've got to learn to fight for your points instead of expecting easy victories. I figure you and Georges have a conditioning problem, but with you, it might be an attitude problem too."

Pierre Gauthier stared into space and said nothing.

Gilles ordered another lemonade and continued to talk about the team and the upcoming season and, while he spoke, the bartender, Benoit, sized him up.

First, Benoit tried to estimate how old Gilles was, eventually deciding he was probably twenty-one. Next, he tried to guess where Gilles was from, choosing Marseille as Gilles had a southern accent. But the thing that intrigued Benoit most was how Gilles talked to them like a drill sergeant and these men, his recruits. Didn't he realize that each of them was a high-powered forex trader making at least three-hundred grand a year, plus healthy bonuses and share options? So who did the kid think he was?

When Gilles finished talking, four of the five left for the locker room. Only Pierre Gauthier and Gilles remained. Gilles was tempted to chat, but Gauthier was using his smartphone, his face intense and sullen. Gilles sat at the bar and quietly sipped his lemonade.

"Are you new here?" asked Benoit. The bartender was good with people. He had a warm smile, a gentle voice.

"That's right. I just started work today. I'm a new squash coach."

"Where are you from?"

"Toulon."

Benoit chuckled. "I guessed Marseille. I could hear your accent."

"You were close," remarked Gilles.

"I have a cousin stationed in Toulon. He's in the navy."

Gilles nodded. "Toulon's a military town. My dad's a retired colonel, and my mum's a major. My brother was a captain, but he left and became a lawyer. It runs in the family."

Now aware of Gilles' upbringing, Benoit figured he understood his behaviour with the other men. Gilles came from a background of strict rules of orders that were given and obeyed. Of course, it wasn't the real world, but what the hell was?

"And you said your mum's a major?"

"That's right. She's in charge of a programme to recruit women into the French armed forces."

Benoit, who was in his early sixties, shook his head with admiration. "That's pretty good going. I remember when the idea of women in the armed forces wasn't even on the menu."

Gilles shrugged. "Times have changed."

"And why didn't you join the armed forces like the rest of your family?"

"I guess it's because I'm good at racquet sports. My parents figured I'd be wasting my talent in the armed forces."

Benoit nodded. "You must be a pretty good coach and player to be where you are at such a young age.

"I'm twenty-two," said Gilles. "I'm also twenty-two in the world rankings."

"No doubt you'll make the top ten."

"Probably," answered Gilles, frank but not boastful.

Benoit nodded, deciding Gilles was all right. There was a TV over the bar, and Benoit clicked on the news where, coincidentally, Marie Sinclair appeared. She was as beautiful as ever, but on-screen struck Gilles as more feminine and polished. Must be the makeup, he thought.

"I saw Marie Sinclair here today," said Gilles.

Benoit nodded. "Yeah. She comes to the club a lot."

For the first time, Gilles smiled. "She makes the news worth watching."

Pierre Gauthier had put away his smartphone and was watching too.

*

After leaving the bar, Gilles went down to the car park, walked to the bike rack, put on his helmet and unlocked his mountain bike. He mounted and glided by the luxury cars and the swimming pool. By the gate, Gilles waved goodbye to the security guards.

Gilles entered the Parisian streets and began a leisurely ride home, taking in his new city, which was familiar and strange for him. He had been there before, but only for short visits. He hadn't even been up the Eiffel tower.

In Paris, the people moved fast, talked quickly, dressed better. They were more sophisticated. The women made quick, flirtatious smiles, then vanished. There were a lot more immigrants.

*

Gilles' flat was in Montmartre, across from a pizzeria and above a barber shop. It was 55 square metres, modern and clean, with a small balcony he liked to sit on.

The lift was small, so Gilles hauled his bike to the second floor and left it in the living room. He then slumped on the sofa, took a deep breath, and summed up his eventful day: the contract with Élan, the men from Dynamic Finance, both crucial to his future. If all went well, he would find his niche in Paris.

He had even seen Marie Sinclair, albeit from a distance.

Gilles was tempted to call his parents but chose not to. Instead, he turned on his laptop and wrote three quick emails: one to his adored older brother, his mother, and his father, telling them that all was well, and his thoughts were with them.

Gilles opened Facebook, read some posts his friends had made, and then began surfing for Marie Sinclair, who actually had a Facebook account, but he learned little about her. There was only one photo.

Gilles left Facebook and went to Wikipedia, which told him more. Born in Lyon, raised in Paris, she came from a wealthy media family. Marie majored in media studies at the Université de Paris and began her career in radio before moving to TV. It even mentioned that she was into squash. Marie Sinclair had just turned thirty.

Apparently, she was involved with a media mogul called Simon Grenier, but there were rumours the relationship had ended.

Gilles kept surfing until he found a bikini shot of Marie Sinclair. He undid his trousers and began to masturbate.

*

With the morning sun shining through his east window, Gilles rose at nine o'clock sharp, drank a half litre of water, and had a breakfast consisting of six egg whites, a large bowl of oatmeal, a banana, and a glass of orange juice. He then relaxed for 27 minutes before taking his bike downstairs and headed for Élan. It took him 21 minutes to get to the club, where he stopped at the gate to show his I.D. He then entered the locker room and adorned a fresh Tee-shirt plus a pair of sweatpants.

Gilles left the locker room and went up to the gym. First, he began his work-out on a step machine before doing a series of weight training exercises: squats, lateral pulls, wrist curls, triceps, a regime designed for squash players. After which, he spent 30 minutes on a stationary bike. He then went on court for a ghosting session, holding his racquet while running from corner to corner pretending to hit a squash ball.

He paused to rest, and at noon Monique Guérin arrived, wearing shorts and a blue Élan Tee-shirt. Her blond hair was tied back, and she was wearing safety glasses as, unlike tennis or badminton, squash is played in a room. No net separates the players.

"How are you today?" she asked.

"All right."

"So, what have you been up to?"

Gilles told her about his training, and she nodded gravely as it was her job to prepare Gilles for an exhibition match against a highly-ranked English player named Mike Stafford. At 33, Stafford was world number three, but his age meant he was on his way out.

Gilles was just the opposite. He was young and climbing like an eagle.

The match was in two weeks' time.

"Okay. Let's get to work," said Monique.

They began with a short game that Gilles won easily, but it allowed Monique to observe his progress.

"Okay," said Monique. "You're moving well, but you still have a tendency to be a trifle too conservative. You should play more drop shots as Mike Stafford tends to stumble under pressure at the front of the court." Gilles nodded. "Remember: at your level, points are scored and lost at the front of the court. Your opponent will almost always be able to return from the back and will almost never hit the ball high and out. "

"Sure," said Gilles. He had been told this before, but he was naturally conservative.

"With your speed, you'll have no problem keeping up to Mike Stafford and might even be able to wear him down. "

Monique was sweating, drops following from her body onto the wood floor. She was also speaking loudly as the other courts were occupied, and it wasn't easy talking over the din of people playing squash.

"Okay, I think we should practise cross-court volley drops, from right to left. Go to the T." Gilles went to the T at the court centre and Monique to the left of the court. From there, she lifted the ball high to Gilles' right, forcing him to move right, stretch, and then hit the ball low to the left side.

"Try not to be too obvious," said Monique. "Don't be afraid to wrist the ball. The key is that he can't anticipate the shot."

Gilles moved left and volley-dropped right several times, often landing the ball in the nick, where the floor and sidewall joined, causing the ball to bounce at a sharp, unpredictable angle.

"Pretty good," said Monique. "You're playing well."

"Now we should practise returning straight volley drops because that's how Mike Stafford gets a lot of points. You hit a loose shot, and he can kill you."

Monique told Gilles to hit a loose shot from the back of the court, after which she volleyed the ball low, straight, and tight to the wall. Gilles raced to the T and then lurched forward, managing a weak return.

"Try to lob the ball," said Monique.

Gilles and Monique repeated the exercise until Gilles was proficiently getting to and returning the ball.

"Good work," said Monique. "Try to practise that one your own."

"I will," promised Gilles.

Gilles and Monique parted company. Gilles went to the locker room, showered, then walked to The Last Serve to have lunch and a lemonade. He sat in the corner where a window overlooked the squash courts. He watched the people below, pounding the ball, shouting and running, releasing stress, which Gilles figured was the best part of squash. He had been playing since he was seven.

Gilles was still munching his herring and pasta salad when he noticed Marie Sinclair enter the squash section. She was wearing a white tee-shirt and grey shorts. Her long black hair was in a ponytail. She strode onto her court and, after the ball was warm, began hitting backhand drives. Gilles watched closely, noting that she hit the ball well. No doubt she could handle most men.

He only wished more women played squash and then wondered if he could find a more revealing photo of Marie Sinclair.

*

The afternoon drifted on, and Gilles went for his second training session with Dynamic Finance, forcefully marching toward the four men assembled in the squash section, which contained twelve courts.

"Good afternoon, gentleman." he said curtly. "How are you today?"

"Fine," said Jean-Luc de Beaumais, answering for all of them.

"Where's Pierre Gauthier?" asked Gilles.

There were a few shrugs after which they mumbled their ignorance. Gilles grimaced. In squash, punctuality was a must as courts were booked by the hour. Also, the Dynamic training sessions were geared for five players: three booked courts, two used by four players, while Gilles used the third for individual coaching.

Gauthier's absence meant he had to alter the training plan.

"Well, I guess we should get going."
Gilles began with a running/ghosting drill, two men to each court. Holding their racquet, they had to run from the centre of the court to a front corner, back to the T, then to a back corner. One man ran on the left side, the other on the right.

Gilles slowly modelled the necessary footwork, explaining that efficient court coverage was one of the keys to successful squash.

Gilles clapped his hands. "Ok. Each guy - 15 corners. Get going!"

It wasn't easy, but they did their best, something Gilles appreciated. He also observed that they enjoyed the individual challenge yet worked together.

"Okay. Two minutes, rest, then change sides."

The men gasped and panted, but when the two minutes expired, they resumed running. It was then Pierre Gauthier arrived.

"Where were you?" Gilles demanded.

Gauthier was a tallish man with thinning brown hair and thick glasses. Although slim, there was still something slack, even weak, about him. He seemed bothered and resentful.

"I was finishing some work," he explained.

"Punctuality is a must," insisted Gilles. "Don't let it happen again."

Gauthier glared at him with a slightly veiled mixture of envy and contempt. Envy because Gilles was a genius with a squash racquet, and no matter how hard he tried, Gauthier could never be that good. Contempt because Gilles was not an élite school yuppie and, compared to Gauthier, didn't make much money.

"Let's get moving," said Gilles.

Gilles told Rachid Naziz to come out and had Gauthier start the running drill, watching to see if he would do it. Unlike the other men, the effort was half-hearted. Gilles wondered why he had joined the squash team.

The two hours passed quickly and, as before, Gilles and the tired team trooped up to The Last Serve where, in the true French style, Gilles openly praised and criticized individual players, admiring their guts but berating them for their inadequacies with particular attention paid to Pierre Gauthier, his lateness, his lack of fitness, and his attitude problem.

After he was finished, four of the five went to the locker room while Pierre Gauthier remained in the bar, glaring down at his smartphone. This time Gilles didn't even think about chatting with him.

"How are you today?" asked Benoit.

"Fine." Gilles had ordered a large lemonade and was sitting at the counter. "No complaints."

"Good to hear it."

Benoit nodded. If Gauthier hadn't been there, he would have suggested that Gilles ease up on the criticism, reminding him that they were his clients. However, Gilles would have replied that, in fact, Dynamic Finance paid for the coaching, and the company expected a total effort.

Benoit turned on the eight o'clock news, but Marie Sinclair didn't appear. Instead, there was a male announcer.

Gilles smiled and sighed. "No Marie tonight."

Pierre Gauthier had ceased watching.

*

With Pierre Gauthier, things went from bad to worse. The next session, he arrived late and, despite Gilles' annoyance, left early, missing the post-training talk in the bar. With an angry frown, Gilles watched him leave, vowing to give him just one more chance.

*

But Gauthier did not change his ways, arriving late, stopping to talk on his mobile, and getting into an argument with Jacques Bertrand and Rachid Naziz. The other men disliked him, which made things easier

In the bar, Gilles was more diplomatic, polite and optimistic than before. He talked of their potential and put them in ranking order.

"Jean-Luc, I'd say, right now, you're our number one guy. The best on the team. You seem to be more focused now, your shots are good, and you've got good fitness. Sometimes you tend to hang back a bit too much, but that's improving."

Clearly pleased, Jean-Luc blushed and looked down at his hands, which prompted Gilles to smile.

Gilles looked over at Georges Lanthier. "Georges, you'll be our number two guy. Your fitness has improved slightly, and so has your patience. Your volleys are good, and you'll be fine if you keep hitting the ball deep, but don't try too many drop shots."

Georges Lanthier nodded and smiled.

Gilles continued the ranking order, placing Jacques Bertrand number three, Pierre Gauthier number four, and Rachid Naziz at five. Gilles explained that, basically, they were closely matched and that they shouldn't take the team ranking too seriously as it could change.

They thanked him for the lesson, and four out of five went to the locker room. As usual, Pierre Gauthier stayed in the bar, scowling at his telephone, sending text messages, reminding Gilles of a sulking child. Gilles had never once seen him smile.

"Like another lemonade?" asked Benoit.

"Why not?"

Benoit's dexterous fingers mixed the drink, which he handed to Gilles.

"So, how's it going?" asked Benoit.

"All right."

"You've already been here two weeks."

"That's right."

"And you've got a big match coming up?" asked Benoit.

"This Saturday."

"Good luck."

The clock on the wall read 19:58. The summer sun was starting to set. Benoit took the remote and clicked on the TV. Gilles noticed that Pierre Gauthier had set down his mobile and was glued to the screen.

Marie Sinclair appeared.

*

After a restless night, filled with dreams of bouncing balls and Marie Sinclair, Gilles rose and right away phoned Céline de Vasseur, his contact at Dynamic Finance.

"Céline," he said. "It's Gilles. You know, the squash coach."

"Hi, Gilles. How's it going?"

"I guess all right, but I've got a problem with one of the guys on the Dynamic team."

"Really? Who's that?"

"Pierre Gauthier. "

"Pierre Gauthier. Oh, yeah. I know him. So, ah, what's the problem?"

"He's causing trouble. He constantly comes late, leaves early, and stops to talk on his mobile. Also, his heart isn't into it. He only makes a half effort, and the other guys are starting to resent him."

"Have you talked to him?" asked Céline.

"Sure, but it hasn't made any difference." Of course, Gilles' idea of talking meant giving orders and reprimands, but Céline got the picture.

"Gilles, I'll tell you what I'll do."

"What's that?"

"I'll phone one or two of the other guys on the team and take it from there. All right?"

"Okay… I guess." Gilles had hoped Dynamic would throw Gauthier off the team then and there. "All right. Call me later."

"I'll do that."

*

Céline de Vasseur informed Gilles that Pierre Gauthier had been taken off the team and was looking for a replacement.

Gilles thanked Céline for her help.

*

For the exhibition match, a special court had been set up. Made for TV, the floor was reddish-brown, the two side walls sky blue, the front wall green with transparent spaces for video cameras. The front wall also displayed the Dynamic Finance logo, the tournament's principal sponsor. The back wall remained clear and transparent.

Around the court, the bleachers were already full. Gilles' coach, Monique Guérin, was sitting in the front row, wearing dark trousers and an Élan Tee-shirt. Gilles glanced into the crowd and saw that all four members of the Dynamic squash team were there, which inspired him.

Some fanfare preceded the match, with the announcer stressing that Gilles was French and from Toulon, which summoned a loud cheer. Mike Stafford was introduced as English from Birmingham, which brought polite applause.

*

The match began with each player feeling the other out, mostly straight and cross-court drives, some lobs, not too many drop shots. Gilles was careful not to hit high and straight to his forehand to minimize Stafford's volley drop. Everything was going well.

Gradually Gilles started playing more offensively, driving Stafford deep and picking him off with cross-court volley drops. Thanks to training with Monique Guérin, he was returning well, limiting Stafford's strengths. In addition, Gilles realized he was slightly faster than Stafford and could match his endurance. In the noisy crowd, he could hear Monique shouting: "Come on, Gilles! Come on!"

He won the first game, 11-5.

To call the match a thriller would have been an exaggeration. It was primarily methodical, long rallies, waiting for openings, then clever shots, usually followed by good returns, but young Gilles was getting the better of Mike

Stafford, matching his shot-making ability, putting on pressure, forcing him to make mistakes.

Gilles won the second game 11-7.

"Come on, Gilles!" shouted Monique. "Come on!"

During the brief break, Monique came to talk to him:

"Don't let up. Don't sit back and wait for him to tire out or make mistakes. Just keep the pressure on."

And Gilles did just that. Despite the Englishman's ferocious, almost kamikaze effort, Gilles continued the onslaught, winning the third game 11-6.

When Stafford lost the last point on an unforced error, the partisan crowd broke into applause, a few, perhaps drunk, actually bellowing the French national anthem. Gilles left the court, threw his arms around Monique Guérin, waved, and smiled at the forex boys.
There was a brief closing ceremony at which Gilles was given a cheque for six thousand euros. Stafford received three.

Gilles was even asked to sign a few autographs because he was now a celebrity in the narrow world of professional squash.

*

That evening Gilles didn't hurry home, instead resting by the Seine to watch the sun's soft rays caress the romantic river. Couples-gay and straight-were strolling hand in hand. On barges, people were going about their business.

Sitting on a bench, Gilles took out his mobile and saw that his mum and brother had called. First, he returned his mum's call.

"Congratulations, Gilles. You were brilliant. We're so proud."

"Did you see the match?"

"Of course. It was live on Squash TV. Your dad and I both watched it. Your brother too."

"Is Marc there?" Gilles adored his older brother.

"Yes. He's here too. We watched it together."

"Great," answered Gilles.

He subsequently talked to his dad and brother and, after hanging up, longed to be back in Toulon with his family.

*

The afternoon following his victory against Mike Stafford, the luxurious Élan locker room was crowded with the after-work crowd preparing for tennis, squash, and badminton.

Most were well-paid businesspeople who wanted a quick sweat before heading home.
Mainly they discussed work, but sometimes sports and politics. Seldom discussed were women and family.

That day, as usual, Gilles entered the locker room quietly, sat down, and began to dress for his session with Dynamic Finance. By now, he recognized the regulars, and they recognized him. A couple even came forward and congratulated him on his match. Gilles just smiled and shook their hands, modestly saying merci. But he didn't try to socialize because he felt out of his element and wasn't sure what to say. Still, most seemed like decent, hard-working blokes, only better paid than the average.

But that day, Gilles was startled by the arrival of Pierre Gauthier, whom he had thrown off the Dynamic Finance squash team. When he saw Gauthier, he looked down, hoping to ignore him, but was nonplussed when Gauthier, sporting a friendly smile, approached him, leaned over, and touched his shoulder.

"Gilles, I heard about your match against Mike Stafford, and I want to express my heartfelt congratulations."

"Ah, thanks."

Gauthier was dressed in an expensive suit with a light-yellow tie. He wasn't carrying an equipment bag, so he obviously wasn't there to play squash. Had he expressly come to talk to him?

"Apparently, you were magnificent."

"It went well. Thanks a lot."

Gauthier stopped smiling. "Gilles, there's something I want to say."

"Sure. Okay."

"Gilles, I'd like to apologize for my behaviour on the squash team. I wasn't a good team player, and I think it's all for the best that I'm no longer part of it." Gauthier's voice was calm, almost serene. His brown eyes were looking straight at Gilles.

"Okay."

Gauthier extended his hand, which Gilles hesitantly shook.

"I wish you and the guys all the best and, I hope, there are no hard feelings."

"No. Of course not."

Gauthier bowed slightly, half smiled, and headed for the door, waving quickly just before he disappeared. Gilles wasn't sure what to think.

*

Now that Pierre Gauthier was gone, the Dynamic Finance session was a lot easier. Each team member arrived promptly and carefully followed Gilles' instructions, giving him a chance to focus on individual improvement. In the end, he had two men play a game, and the other two observe, asking them to note the errors they had seen.

Gilles saw their happy, determined expressions. A team was being built, and he liked Dynamic's chances in the upcoming corporate league competitions.

There was still no word from Céline de Vasseur about a replacement for Gauthier.

*

It was almost eight in the evening when Gilles left the club. The August sun was low in the west, and there was a stiff northern breeze, but it was still way too early to think about winter.

Gilles unlocked his mountain bike and was about to mount when, out of the clear blue, came a woman's voice.

"You were wonderful!'

Not knowing who it was, Gilles turned and found himself facing Marie Sinclair, who seemed almost an apparition right then.

Tossed by the wind, her long black hair a touch messy. She was wearing a patterned grey dress that reached her knees and hugged her body in a way that enhanced her curves. On her feet, she had white shoes, and she was holding a dark leather handbag. If Gilles had known anything about fashion and cosmetics, he would have known her outfit cost three grand. Maybe more.

Her perfume, coaxed by the breeze, was enticing.

Her pink, vaguely Asian face was beaming with pleasure.

"Wonderful!" she repeated.

"Thank you," Gilles said. He reckoned she was talking about the match against Mike Stafford but wasn't sure.

She laughed. "Of course, I'm talking about your match on Saturday."

"You saw it?"

"I watched it on Squash TV."

She continued smiling, then came closer, extending her neck to show she wanted to kiss him on both cheeks. Gilles leaned forward and felt her lips touch first his right cheek, then his left.

"Congratulations," she said.

Blushing, Gilles just nodded and smiled. He hadn't a clue what to say but thankfully didn't need to say anything as Marie Sinclair continued with a gushing cheerleader charm that many guys, including Gilles, fell for.

She went on about the match, admiring how Gilles had decimated the Anglais, forcing the Anglais deep until the Anglais didn't know if he was coming or going, and it was great when the Anglais lost three straight. Listening to her, Gilles felt like he had become a French national hero, right up there with Jeanne d'Arc and Charles de Gaulle.

"So, what are you up to now?" she asked.

"Me? I'm on my way home."

"Well, maybe we could go somewhere?"

Her expression was warm and inviting, and Gilles was hardly inclined to say no. "Sure. Wherever you like… Maybe we could go for a walk by the Seine."

"That would be nice, but, you know, I want to avoid publicity. So maybe we could go somewhere a bit more secluded."

Gilles wasn't about to argue. "Sure, but what about my bike?"

"No problem. You can put it in the trunk of my car."

Marie Sinclair was driving a cherry red Mercedes sedan and Gilles, who knew more about cars than fashion, was impressed. He put his bike in the trunk, then climbed into the passenger seat, ready for what was sure to be a memorable night.

The powerful car purred to life and drove through the gate where Gilles, as usual, waved to the security guards.

All the while, Marie Sinclair was smiling and, when they stopped at a red light, she reached over and squeezed his hand.

Gilles couldn't believe his luck.

*

After a couple of drinks in a dark Pigalle jazz bar, they ended up at Gilles' Montmartre apartment.

"It's no palace," he said. "But it suits me just fine."

Marie Sinclair looked around a bit but then approached, wrapped her arms around him, and started kissing him.

"I want you," she whispered.

Now, although only twenty-two, Gilles already needed four hands to count his women. This was partially due to good looks as he was tall, slim, and muscular with curly dark hair offset by sharp blue eyes, but that didn't make him seductive. He lacked the gift of the gab, a reservoir of clever lines, and was far from romantic. He was inevitably honest, straightforward, and nice with women, which were not always winning traits for a seducer.

Rather Gilles' success was due to his mother's job. She was responsible for recruiting young women into the French armed forces, which meant Gilles had access to a steady stream of females. In fact, his lovers had all been prospective recruits, the oldest twenty-one.

Marie Sinclair was different. At thirty, she was older, way more sophisticated, and Gilles wasn't sure what to expect.

In bed, Marie sure knew what she was doing. She had every move, every position, every touch down pat. Yet throughout it all, her face held a friendly yet determined look, as if she was trying hard to please, and even when they were doing it, Gilles was surprised how selfless she was. Gilles had always figured women were in it for themselves.

Around three in the morning, she ruffled his hair. "Gotta go."

"Okay."

"However, I'll be in the squash courts tomorrow a bit after four. Wait for me, and you can come and say hello."

"I'll do that."

"I'll give you a call," she said.

Gilles heaved a deep sigh, hoisted himself from bed, went to the fridge, and helped himself to a drink of apple juice from a stiff paper container. He then looked in the mirror, shook his head, and smiled.

"Jesus Christ," he said to himself. "You did it with Marie Sinclair."

For most men sleeping with a TV beauty would be an exploit, and Gilles was no exception. But Gilles differed in that he wouldn't brag about it, and he had his father to thank for that.

When Gilles was eight, he and his older brother, Marc, had been in the living room with their father, who, in full uniform, was sitting in an armchair drinking brandy, no doubt a bit drunk.

"Boys," he said. "I've got something to say to you." Gilles' dad was fond of making father/son talks, most often impromptu, and inspired by brandy.

"A real man never brags about getting fucked." The boys didn't reply, but Marc looked down and stifled a laugh.

"Don't laugh, Marc," retorted his father. "Because it's no joke. Only a jackass brags about his sex life."

From that day, Gilles had followed his dad's advice, never boasting about his women. It was a lesson that would serve him well.

Gilles returned to bed and relived the evening's events, starting with meeting Marie at the bike rack and how, out of the clear blue, she had come forward and talked to him. After that, it was like a whirlwind: the cherry red Mercedes, the Pigalle jazz bar, the trip to his place, and then sex. Almost too good to be true.

Another man, perhaps deeper and wiser, might have asked himself a few questions, but Gilles wasn't another man. So instead, he imagined Marie moving on top of him and, only briefly, wished she had been just a little shy, a bit clumsy, a tad more natural.

Gilles closed his eyes and drifted off to sleep.

*

His mind foggy from the previous night's drinks, Gilles awakened to a beautiful Parisian morning. Sparrows were chirping, and people were already bustling in the street. He yawned and entered the kitchen, making a pot of strong espresso before eating his usual breakfast.

He rode quickly to Élan and, when entering the club's gates, showed his identification to the security guard named Gaston.

"So, how'd you make out with that woman?" Gaston asked, grinning.

"What woman?"

"The one I saw you with here with last night. She looked a lot like Marie Sinclair."

Gilles half smiled but didn't answer, just taking back his I.D. and riding to the bike rack. Then, he dismounted and went into the club.

It was late morning, the locker room almost empty. Only a few men he didn't know were there, likely casual players getting ready to play squash. At first, Gilles didn't pay them any mind, but one, short and muscular, approached him.

"Are you Gilles Leclerc?"

"That's right."

"I'm Stéphane Boisvert." He extended his hand, which Gilles shook.

"What can I do for you, Stéphane?"

"Nothing really. I just wanted to congratulate you on your big win."

They had posted the match results by the main entrance, along with his photo, but it surprised him that a complete stranger would come over and praise him.

"Thanks."

He then gave Gilles a coy, knowing smile. "So, what's this rumour about you and Marie?"

Gilles frowned. "What rumour?"

113

"Apparently, she and you are now an item."
He was smirking in a way that made Gilles want
to punch him in the face. He could tell the other
men were listening.

"I have no clue what you're talking about. "

"Oh. Come on."

But Gilles just ignored him, hurriedly
dressed, and left the locker room.

*

That day Gilles worked out harder than usual,
angry at himself for drinking in a Pigalle Bar and
staying up late, which interfered with his
training. Also, he was puzzled and anxious
about the rumours. No doubt some people had
seen him with Marie outside the club and then
get into her car, but so what?

Had Marie actually told someone, or was it
just silly gossip? The picture wasn't right.

*

After lunch, Gilles gave two lessons to a
couple of club members, showered, then
returned to the court area to wait for Marie. His
watch read 15:50. He felt nervous and thought
about just going home and forgetting about
Marie Sinclair. But, after all, Gilles reckoned a

one-night stand was often better than a short affair.

Gilles sat on a chair and commenced watching a squash match between two veteran players until he saw Marie arrive. He smiled and started to get up, but her disdainful look warned him not to do so.

Gilles stayed put and let her approach, observing a far different woman than the purring sex bomb from the night before. First of all, her clothes were simple: white jeans and a blue Université de Paris Tee-shirt. No make-up. She was carrying an equipment bag and looked in a rush.

When she was close, Gilles smiled and said hello, but she brushed by him like he didn't exist, leaving Gilles to wonder where she had found her movie star strut, her top-model stride? Gilles went to a window and saw her cross the car park. She climbed into a white Volkswagon Golf and drove away.

*

And yet that very evening, she sent him a text message.

Gilles, I loved our night together and want to see you again. What about tomorrow night at your place? About nine? Kisses, Marie.

Gilles replied: Okay. See you then.

*

Tomorrow came, and Gilles followed his usual routine: Up early, breakfast, coffee, then off to Élan to train in the half-empty gym as it was now late August and a lot of Parisians were on holiday, basking on a Spanish beach or further afield.

As he was upstairs pumping iron, he thought of his family and wished for a quick trip to Toulon, but he had too many squash commitments. Another exhibition match was coming up, and Monique Guérin stressed that his win against Mike Stafford didn't mean that much.

"You're only as good as your next match. Keep training hard."

And, of course, Gilles did: weight training, step machine, court training. He also had scheduled lessons and his sessions with Dynamic Finance, who, for some reason, hadn't gone on holiday.

It was only a bit after three, so Gilles had some time before his session with Dynamic. He went down to court level and contemplated using an open court for some stretching, but he wasn't in the mood and, quite frankly, felt like doing nothing. So, Gilles settled in a chair, relaxed, actually dozing off, and just when he was starting to dream of his brother, Gilles had a strange awakening, which would mark him for life.

"Excuse me. Are you Gilles?"

Startled, Gilles jerked awake and looked up to see Marie peering down at him. She was wearing squash clothes and holding a racquet.

She smiled. "Are you Gilles Leclerc?"

Of course, Gilles was confused and luckily tongue-tied, so he didn't say something sarcastic like *That's right. You know, I'm the guy you fucked just the other night.* Instead, he gave her a peculiar look, which she interpreted as shyness.

"Sorry for having woken you up, but are you the squash coach, Gilles Leclerc?"

Gilles continued to give her a peculiar stare, actually scratching his head with puzzlement.

"Have you talked to Céline?"

Gilles managed to say: "Céline de Vasseur?"

"That's right."

"Ah, no. I haven't spoken to her. Why?"

"Okay then… You don't know. Anyway, Céline told me there was an opening on the Dynamic Finance squash team and asked if I would fill in."

"Really?"

Marie Sinclair's lovely smile disappeared, now assuming that Gilles didn't want a woman on the team, but thankfully Gilles' pulled himself together.

"Oh, okay," he said. "Great. Welcome to the team."

"I'm Marie." She extended her hand, which Gilles happily shook.

"Of course, I know who you are. I've also seen you playing squash, and you look like you're a good player."

"Thank you." Her smile had returned.

"Anyway, Marie, the other guys aren't here yet. Maybe we could hit the ball a bit and play a short game?"

"Sure."

So, Gilles became Marie Sinclair's squash coach. They stepped on the court and began to practise: straight drives, boasts and drives, and volleys. They then played a game, and Gilles recognized that Marie was a tough competitor, foul-mouthed and determined, shouting *putain* when she missed a shot, which prompted him to smile, and realize she was a far cry from the woman he had slept with.

"Keep you racquet up," he shouted. "Turn your body toward the wall."

While they were playing, Gilles discreetly checked her out. There was a thin, jagged scar on her right knee, maybe from a dog bite or broken glass. On her left ankle was a small blackbird tattoo. She hadn't shaved her legs.

"Okay, Marie. Let's take a break."

Marie was sweating and leaned against the wall. Gilles took a chart from his equipment bag and made notes about her game: her strong and weak points. His main concern was her endurance. Could she run with the guys?

"Okay," he said. "As I said, you're a pretty good player."

Gilles was about to say more, but then the rest of the team arrived: Jean-Luc, Georges, Jacques, and Rachid. Gilles saw they were surprised, even flustered by the unexpected presence of a beautiful, well-known woman.

"Good afternoon, gentlemen," began Gilles. "Before we begin, let me introduce the newest member of our team, Marie Sinclair." He studied their reactions. "Does anyone not know her?"

Marie smiled at them and nodded.

"Of course, we know her," said Rachid, who was the easiest with people of the four. "But you also work as a media consultant at Dynamic, right?"

"That's right," said Marie. "Céline de Vasseur told me there was an opening on the team and asked me to fill in. I know the team is supposed to be for forex staff, so I hope you don't mind."

"Of course not," replied Rachid. "Welcome aboard." The others smiled and graciously welcomed her.

The practice went well, Marie exhibiting superior racquet skills and speed, which compensated for her lack of endurance.

Afterwards, in the bar, Gilles gave his usual post-training talk.

"Marie," he said. "I think I'll put you in the number three spot. You've got excellent racquet skills. My big concern is your endurance. Do you do any other training besides squash?" She shook her head. "Well, it might be a good idea to do some long-distance running or work out on a treadmill or a step machine."

"Okay. I'll see what I can do. "

"Also, you're probably pretty busy. Do you think you'll be able to attend practices regularly?"

Marie nodded. "Yeah. No problem. For the next year, all my broadcasts are on weekends, so I'll be able to attend."

"Good," said Gilles, thinking what a radical improvement she was over Pierre Gauthier. "Well, that's it for today. See you all on Tuesday, same time, same place."

The team departed, and Gilles remained in the bar with Benoit.

"Like another lemonade?" asked Benoit.

"Sure."

Benoit mixed the drink and was tempted to kid Gilles about his beautiful TV sweetheart being on the team and how he would now have to mind his manners. However, he didn't because Benoit sensed that something was on Gilles' mind. The latter man was pensive and withdrawn, not his usual self. It wasn't that Gilles seemed unhappy, just trying hard to make sense of a situation.

When the clock clicked to 20:00, Gilles stood up.

"Thanks for the lemonade. I wish I could stay longer, but I'm meeting someone at nine o'clock. Catch you later."

"Sure."

*

Gilles went and sat on the balcony once at home, happy just to stare at the people below. Across the street, the pizzeria was almost full, and on the terrace, a group of young German tourists were drinking beer and laughing. Gilles wished he was down there with them instead of waiting for a woman called Marie Sinclair.

He looked at his watch. It was 8:57, so she was due in three minutes, and Gilles had no idea what to say or do.

A taxi cab pulled up and stopped in front of the pizzeria. From the back seat, a young woman alighted, and Gilles saw that it was her. She opened the front passenger door and passed the driver the fare. The taxi drove off, and she headed toward his building.

She was sporting a classy blue dress that stopped mid-thigh, carrying a white handbag and wearing white shoes. Her hair was perfectly in place.

The doorbell rang. Gilles went to the intercom and asked who it was.

"Marie," she said.

"Come right up."

Gilles didn't open the door, instead waiting for her to knock. Finally, he heard soft footsteps and the sound of long fingernails tapping, after which he let her in.

"Salut," he said.

She entered, and Gilles recognized the same delicious perfume from their first night. Her make-up was perfect, a delicate blush that made her seem soft and daintier than the woman he had played squash with that very afternoon.

Gilles gestured toward the living room. "Come on in."

She grinned and nodded. She then walked into Gilles' small living room and settled on the sofa, likely expecting him to sit beside her, but Gilles took a chair.

"Would you like anything?" he asked.

"No. I'm fine."

Gilles didn't say anything for a bit, his blue eyes studying her smooth and flawless legs.

"You have really nice legs," he remarked.

She half giggled. "Thanks a lot."

"I mean, they're so smooth. No scars, no blotches. Not even a tattoo."

She shrugged. "I guess not."

Gilles' hands were sweating and his underarms wet, but his voice was controlled and calm.

"I especially notice that you don't have a scar on your right knee or a blackbird tattoo on your left ankle."

She gave him a funny look. "No, I don't. Should I?"

Gilles leaned forward. "So, who are you anyway?"

She stiffened, then reddened, like someone who had just been caught shoplifting.

Gilles didn't wait for her to answer. Then, abruptly, he got to his feet and, lightning-quickly, went over and grabbed her handbag, which was lying on the coffee table. Then, still standing, he opened the handbag and emptied it on the coffee table, watching the contents spill and clatter like jellybeans.

Gilles could see she was frightened, her arms crossed over her chest.

He didn't say anything, just squatted down to study the objects on the table. There were cigarettes, Valium, a bag of weed, sleeping pills, and even a shiny wrapper that might have cocaine in it. There were also car keys, a mobile phone, a cigarette lighter, and cosmetics. Next to the mobile phone were two documents: a driver's licence and an identity card.

Gilles picked up the I.D. card and scanned it. "Your name is Fabienne Faubois," he said. "You're thirty-two years old and live in the eighth district. You were born in Paris. The real Marie Sinclair was born in Lyon."

Sighing, Gilles quietly left the I.D. card on the table and returned to his chair. He leaned back and clasped his hands, doing his best to appear peaceful as he didn't want to hurt her, and it bothered him that she was afraid.

"So, what's this all about?" he asked, not sure if he'd get an answer.

Fabienne Faubois frowned. "It was supposed to be a joke." Her voice now sounded raspy and a touch vulgar.

"A joke?"

"Yeah, he said he wanted to play a joke on you."

"Who?"

"Pierre Gauthier."

Gilles nodded, his lips forming a reflective scowl. "Did he say why?"

"He said you were a nobody asshole, just a stupid peasant. He wanted to make an idiot of you." She paused. "Is it okay if I smoke?"

"I guess." Gilles rose and opened the balcony window to let fresh air in, then went into the kitchen and returned with a coffee cup saucer for an ashtray.

She lit a cigarette, and Gilles could tell she was starting to relax. "He didn't exactly say why, but obviously, he doesn't like you."

"Obviously not," replied Gilles. "I had him thrown off the squash team. He's a lazy prick."

Fabienne Faubois nodded. "Anyway, he paid me a thousand euros to sleep with you, hoping you'd believe I was Marie Sinclair."

Gilles whistled. "A thousand euros. Just to sleep with me."

"That's right. He said he'd give me two grand more if everything worked out." She looked bitter.

"So, what did he hope would happen?"

"He was hoping you'd make an idiot of yourself with the real Marie Sinclair. That you'd brag about fucking her, and even go up to her and

125

start kissing and touching her and maybe even fondle her. He was hoping you might even lose your job because of it."

"Sounds pretty far-fetched," remarked Gilles.

"Oh, I don't know. Most guys would at least brag about fucking Marie Sinclair, and why wouldn't you fondle her, especially since you would have figured you'd already fucked her."

Although no puritan, it bothered Gilles to hear a woman talk like that

"I suppose," he agreed, mulling it over. What would have happened if Marie hadn't replaced Gauthier on the Dynamic squash team? Would he ever have twigged?

"And, believe me, if you had bragged about it, Gauthier would have gone straight to the Élan and Dynamic management and complained. That's the kind of prick he is."

Gilles recalled Gauthier's phony apology in the locker room and later the guy who had asked him about Marie.

"The day after we met, a guy in Élan's locker room asked me about Marie Sinclair and me."

Fabienne nodded knowingly. "Did he say what his name was?"

Gilles pondered. "I think he said his name was Boisvert."

"Short, muscular guy?"

"That's right," said Gilles.

"He's one of Gauthier's flunkies. No doubt Gauthier told him to lead you on. But, like I said, he's a real prick."

"Well," Gilles said. "Gauthier's nasty little joke didn't work out. Thank goodness for that."

"No, it didn't." Her voice was glum, probably thinking of the two grand she wouldn't get.

"So where in the hell did Gauthier find you? I mean, you're almost a dead ringer for Marie Sinclair."

She nodded. "I work for an agency."

"A talent agency?"

She smiled at Gilles' naivety. "No, an escort agency. I'm a prostitute."

"I didn't realize that."

"Gauthier's a regular client. He has an obsession with Marie Sinclair. Sometimes he even pays to watch other guys fuck me. Boisvert is one of them."

"Really? Does he even know her?"

She shook her head. "He's tried to talk to her once or twice, but she just brushed him off. I guess she has good taste in men."

"Weird situation," said Gilles.

"Not that weird. I have several clients willing to pay for a Marie Sinclair look-alike. "

"I would never have guessed."

"And maybe you're one of them?" Her smile was coy, and her laugh teasing.

Gilles went scarlet. "I don't think so."

Fabienne Faubois chuckled, then leaned forward and starting putting her stuff back in the handbag. She then stood up.

"By the way, how did you know I wasn't the real Marie Sinclair?"

"Sheer luck, actually. This afternoon I met Marie Sinclair. When it was obvious that she didn't know who I was, I knew something was wrong. So I played squash with her and saw that she had a scar on her right knee and a tattoo on her left ankle."

"I see," she mumbled. "Anyway, I'm off."

"Sure. Okay."

Fabienne Faubois left without saying goodbye.

*

Gilles helped himself to apple juice, then sat on the balcony, quietly watching the street below. In the pizzeria, the Germans were gone, and now there were two young women and an elderly couple who seemed to be arguing.

Gilles shook his head and scowled. He had been the victim of a cruel and extravagant practical joke and could hardly believe that some yuppie prick would go to such lengths to make him look stupid. Wow, he thought. Welcome to Paris.

He returned to the kitchen for more apple juice, then went back to the balcony. The elderly couple were leaving, but the two young women were still there. One of them smiled and waved, and Gilles waved back. The other beckoned for him to come down.

Gilles reminded himself that he was young and free, and it was fantastic living in Paris.

David and Imre

"Whatever happened to David Spencer?"

It was late afternoon. The bar at the City Racquets Club was almost empty, just Dale and Wendy drinking lemonade and talking old times after a game of doubles squash.

"Nobody knows for sure," answered Wendy. "Basically, he just disappeared."

Dale and Wendy were sitting by a window. Across the street was Vancouver's Queen Elizabeth Park with its green slopes, conservatory, and lush flowerbeds.

Dale frowned. "Yeah. It happened just after Imre died. David came in, cleaned out his locker, and left. Nobody heard from him again."

The bartender, Frank, was standing with his arms crossed. He also remembered David, an orange juice drinker. Imre had been a vodka man.

"I heard he was screwing Imre's wife," said Dale.

Wendy rolled her eyes. Dale was always telling stupid gossip. Probably he figured it made him more interesting.

To change the subject, Wendy said, "He was an excellent squash player."

Dale nodded, "That's for sure. Wicked backhand. Great reflexes. He could run forever."

"You ever beat him?"

Dale shook his head, a kind of helplessness crossing his face. "Not even close. I almost won a game once but lost 9-7. I was ahead 7-2, but he came roaring back. All told, I must have played him ten times and never even won a single game. But, Christ, he was good."

Dale's voice was devoid of admiration. Instead, he sounded tired, almost fatalistic. He was sixty, a trifle overweight, and had long ago surrendered to doubles squash, a graveyard for worn-out singles players.

Wendy smiled. "Probably we'll never know."

*

In the spring of '83, Imre Horvath joined City Racquets Club. Driving an Audi Quattro, he parked under a flowering dogwood, alighted, and locked the door. Then, after smoothing his hair, he walked to the front entrance and rang the bell. The door clicked open. Inside, a sign said the office was upstairs.

There he was greeted by the receptionist, Nancy Wong. "Can I help you?"

"I want to buy a squash membership," said Imre. He had a light Hungarian accent.

"Sure. Any idea what category?"

Imre shrugged. "What categories are there?"

"Well, here we offer only yearly memberships. There's out of town for people who live outside Vancouver and only come here a few times a year. Then there's a daytime membership, which is good from midnight until four in the afternoon. And then there's a full-time membership which allows you to play whenever you want. I should add that at CRC, there are no court charges. Your membership covers it all."

"Sounds good," said Imre, "I guess I'll take a full-time membership."

"Great." Nancy Wong then smiled like a nurse about to deliver bad news. "However, there is also a five-hundred-dollar initiation fee."

"Okay." Imre took out his cheque book and flipped it open. "Who should I make this out to?"

"You can make it out to CRC. In total, it comes to one thousand dollars."

Imre studiously wrote the cheque, then handed it to Nancy Wong. "Do I have to provide any info?"

She handed him an application form across the counter, which Imre quickly filled out with a gold pen.

"Thank you," said Nancy Wong. "If you want, I can show you around the club."

"Very kind of you, but it's not necessary. However, I am interested in taking some squash lessons."

"Okay… Well, our instructor, David Spencer, is here right now. Would you like to meet him?"

"Certainly."

"Follow me."

Imre followed her down a corridor to a little office adjoining the fitness room. Nancy knocked on the door, then opened it.

"Hi, David."

"Hi, Nancy. How's it going?"

"Fine. David, I'd like you to meet Imre Horvath. He just joined the club and says he's interested in taking squash lessons."

"Okay," David smiled.

Nancy departed.

David nodded at Imre. He then half stood and shook his hand, beckoning for him to take a seat.

"So, you want to take squash lessons?"

Imre nodded. At first glance, David seemed earnest, even grim, but his voice was cheerful and light. He had reddish-brown hair, a decent beard, and blue eyes. He was tall, wiry like you'd expect a squash player to be. He might have been twenty-three.

"That's right," said Imre. "I'm an architect, and some of my colleagues suggested that I play squash."

"I see. How long have you been playing?"

"I've never played before."

"Really?"

Imre was in his late forties. Average height, he had grey hair, a slight paunch. He appeared tired, a bit bleary and distant. His clothes were expensive, and he had a Rolex watch.

"That's right. I'm a complete beginner."

David half frowned and, for a brief moment, considered telling Imre to forget it because he was too old to start squash. He needed something less intense, less demanding, but necessity held him back: David needed the money.

"Well, I guess we can arrange that. How many lessons do you want?"

"Well, maybe three times a week."

David hesitated. His late afternoon slots were all filled. "What time of day?"

"I'm actually flexible. My work allows me to come and go as I please. So late mornings would be good."

"About eleven?"

"Eleven would be good. Maybe Monday, Wednesday, and Thursday."

"Sounds good. And have you any idea how many lessons you want?"

Imre pondered a bit. "I guess a year's worth."

"A year's worth." David calculated how much money he could make. "That's a lot of lessons."

Imre didn't comment

"Okay, I'll tell you what," David pursued. "I think we should agree on 150 lessons."

"All right."

David had seldom met such a compliant client: money no object, no questions, no answers needed.

"I'll have a lawyer draw up a contract. Basically, the contract will stipulate the price per lesson-fifteen dollars an hour-and the time frame that the 150 lessons need to be completed. There will also be a cancellations clause."

"Okay," said Imre.

"When would you like your first lesson?"

"How 'bout this Thursday?"

"Sounds good," said David, now sensing that Imre was eager to start. "Anyway, before that, would you like to have a look around the club?" Imre shrugged. "Why not?"

David and Imre stood and left the office, which David carefully locked.

"Follow me."

And, like an obedient soldier, Imre followed. They entered the squash section, and the sound of people playing, before faint, grew louder and louder. Balls were whacking the walls, people shouting, metal clanging.

David stopped outside an empty squash court, of which the back wall was transparent, the others opaque and painted white.

"As you can see, it is a big rectangle with many red lines, which indicate the playing boundaries of the court. It is 9.75 metres long and 6.4 metres wide. "

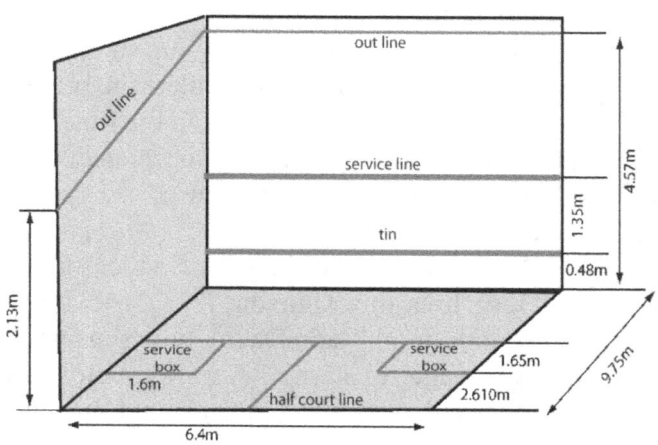

"I see," said Imre.

"At the bottom of the front wall is a long metal strip called the tin, which is the lower out line. The ball makes a loud noise when it hits the tin. The lower red line on the front wall indicates how low you can serve the ball, and the upper red line just indicates how high you can hit the ball without it being out of court."

"Okay."

"Unlike tennis," stressed David. "If the ball hits the line, it's out. "

"I see."

"If you want, we can watch some people play," said David.

"Why not?"

They moved to a court where two people were hammering the small black rubber ball with their long thin racquets.

"As you can probably see, the strategy is to dominate the centre and force your opponent deep and wide, and then, quite often, cut it off and hit a winner at the front of the court."

Thankfully the two players-Dale Hawkins and Wendy Elliot-were good, so the match was entertaining. Imre's blue eyes fixed on the two players, and with acute interest, followed the action.

"How are you fixed for equipment?" asked David.

"I haven't got anything."

"Well, if you want, we can go to the pro shop and check it out."

"Sure," said Imre, all the while watching the match. He seemed reluctant to leave.
They went to the pro shop where a young woman was minding the store.

"I suggest you get a cheap racquet," advised David. "That's because, as a beginner, you're likely to break it soon. Other than that, you need good shoes, shorts and a Tee-shirt. "

David fell silent, letting the shop assistant advise Imre. He was already contemplating their first lesson together, seriously wondering how fit Imre was and how long he'd last. For David, the important thing was for the money to be in his bank account. After that, it didn't matter if Imre quit or not, but David figured he would.

"Oh," said David. "You should also buy safety glasses, too, because you just might get hit in the face."

Imre bought a racquet, fifteen balls, safety glasses, and a good pair of shoes. He paid with an American Express credit card.

The two men then went to the club bar, basically to cement their new relationship. David ordered his usual orange juice, Imre a straight double vodka. The clock over the bar showed six in the evening.

They sat near the long window overlooking the badminton courts where earnest people, primarily Asian, batted shuttlecocks. Every court was occupied, and badminton was quickly overtaking squash as the club's principal sport.

Imre took a long sip of vodka, then set down his glass. "I come from Hungary," he said. "You might have detected my accent."

"That's right, but not at first," said David. "You speak English very well."

"I've been here a long time." Imre nodded. "I arrived in my early twenties."

"Many years."

"I fled Hungary during the Russian invasion in '56. My family comes from a little village called Vácszentlászló, which is close to Budapest. At the time, I was living in Budapest. When I saw the wind change, I made straight for the Austrian border. My family is still over there."

Having taken a course in eastern European history, David was more or less familiar with Hungary.

"Do you go back to visit?"

"Every year," replied Imre.

"That's good," said David. "I'm sure they appreciate it."

139

Imre took another long sip of vodka, staring into the glass as if looking for the solution to some stubborn puzzle. David felt like telling him that alcohol offered no answers but knew better.

In the bar was the usual crowd: Matt Dunn, Bob West, Sarah Miles, Walter Cook, Amir Khan, Ron Bennet, Ray Carter. The majority of the squash players were men, with only a few women sprinkled in. A disproportionate amount of players were also British immigrants, and the squash membership rang with English accents. Most players were in their twenties or thirties because, back in'83, the baby boom was still young. David knew everyone. He had been a club member since he was seven.

Faces still flushed from strenuous exercise, Dale Jenkins and Wendy Elliot arrived,

"Do you have a family?" asked David.

"Yes," answered Imre. "I'm married. I have two sons, Mark and Peter. Mark is just finishing law school, and Peter is in his second year at BCIT. He's going to become an ultrasound technician."

"Good idea," said David.

"My wife works as a legal secretary. She's actually a member of this club. She goes to the gym."

David pondered. "I don't think I know her."

"She's tall and blond. Forty-two years old. Her name's Janet."

The image of a tallish woman with a deep voice entered his mind. Yes, he now knew who she was.

"Is she from Hungary?"

"No. Her maiden name was Davies."

"Welsh," remarked David.

"That's right." Imre got to his feet. "Would you excuse me for a moment?"

"No problem."

David assumed Imre was going to the toilet, but instead, he walked out to the sundeck. David watched him reach into his shirt pocket, then light a cigarette. As he smoked, he slowly paced back and forth.

David drank some orange juice and sighed. A smoker. Thank God he had taken a first aid course and knew how to help a heart attack victim.

Happy Birthday

On the morning of his eighty-fifth birthday, George Patterson had a very strange dream. He was driving his Lincoln Continental in downtown Vancouver when the road suddenly turned to ice. He began sliding helplessly toward a city bus and, although he desperately pumped the big car's brakes, he continued to slide and hit the bus head-on, fully expecting to die.

But then the bedside radio buzzed, freeing George from his nightmare

"My God," he muttered. "Already that time."

Feeling foggy from the two sleeping pills he had taken the night before, George lay in bed for just a bit, then rose and shuffled into the kitchen, where he turned on the coffee maker. After that, he went into the bathroom, brushed his teeth, and shaved.

George returned to the kitchen and took a box of instant porridge from the cupboard, which he set on the counter. He poured water into a saucepan, turned on the stove, and waited for the water to boil before pouring in a cup of porridge, which he stirred with a large stainless steel spoon.

It only took three minutes and thirty-seven seconds for the porridge to thicken. George removed the pot and lay it on the kitchen table. From the fridge, he fetched milk, grabbed the sugar bowl, and then set to eating his usual breakfast. He swallowed the last spoonful of porridge and drank two cups of brewed coffee, which lifted some of the sleeping pill fog.

Never a man to dither, George entered the living room where his dark suit was hanging on a chair. He removed his pyjama top and carelessly flung it on the floor as if it were worthless trash. Ditto the bottoms. He then slipped on his suit, carefully knotting his navy blue tie in the mirror by the front door.

He adorned his overcoat and tapped the right waist pocket to ensure that the Luger pistol was still there, then left the house, not even bothering to close the door.

Outside George was greeted by driving November rain from a gloomy grey sky. George looked both ways, then crossed Main Street after the heavy traffic had stopped for him. He walked to the bus stop and waited for the Number 3 bus, feeling surprisingly calm.

Down the street, the Number 3 bus was gliding northward, its trolley wires looking like insect antennae. When it arrived, George politely allowed the other passengers to board first. Then, he got on and paid the full adult fare, refusing to use a senior's discount.

143

The Number 3 bus was crowded, and, as often happened, George was the only white passenger, the others mostly of Chinese or Punjabi origin. Many of the passengers were young students looking down at their smartphones.

George edged toward the back of the bus, ignoring the seats reserved for elderly and disabled passengers. He found a place to stand, fingered the Luger pistol, and waited for the inevitable to happen.

And it didn't take long. In fact, George had not been standing there a minute when a petite young woman named Debbie Chan made the fatal error.

"Sir," Debbie said cheerfully. "Would you like to sit down?"

Debbie was a second-year science student at Langara College who hoped to become an ultrasound technician. She also worked part-time at a bakery, but more about her later.

George winced and glared at her as if she had insulted him.

"No, thank you," he announced. "I can stand."

Not knowing what to say, Debbie Chan blushed and tried to smile.

"I don't need your pity," muttered George.

"I'm sorry," said Debbie Chan. "I meant no disrespect."

Again, George glared at her, but then his eyes grew glassy. Finally, he started to talk in a bizarre monotone, as in a faraway dream.

"I used to have a Lincoln Continental," he mumbled. "Dark blue. I bought it brand new for my seventy-fifth birthday."

Debbie Chan smiled nervously and nodded, but George was no longer paying much attention to her.

"A year ago, the bastards took away my driver's licence. All because of some stupid little accident in a parking lot. They gave me some tests and told me I shouldn't be driving at all. They said I couldn't react quickly enough and that I was confused."

Debbie Chan was toying with a button on her leather coat. The other passengers were too busy with their smartphones to listen to an older man's dull raving.

"Of course, it wasn't fair. They had it in for me and had already made their minds up before they even saw me."

The bus stopped at 43rd and Main. Several passengers boarded, one of them jostling George as he walked by, but George was too far gone even to notice.

"I sold the Lincoln to a used car lot, and that's why I'm on this bus."

Debbie Chan nodded, thinking that the elderly gentleman was certainly strange, but it never occurred to her that he might be dangerous.

"As you can see, I'm strong enough to stand. I don't need charity, and I don't need pity."

The Number 3 bus was now approaching Main and 41st. A steady rain was falling, the windshield wipers slapping back and forth. Most of the passengers were carrying umbrellas.

"I'd rather die on my feet than live on my knees," George proclaimed in the same weird monotone.

It was then that George took the Luger from his right pocket and, with a steady hand, raised it to his head and pointed the barrel at his temple.

"This was my older brother's pistol," he said matter-of-factly. "He got it during the Second World War."

Debbie Chan clapped her hands over her mouth and shrieked. Several passengers glanced at her before noticing George and the gun. A few began filming with their smartphones, but George paid no heed.

Instead, he serenely pulled the trigger, splattering blood, flesh, and bone on those around him. He died instantly.

Of course, the lowbrow press loved it, and for a few days, George Patterson was big news. The headlines read Bloody Bus Ride and Main Street Mayhem, and the local TV news made it their lead story for three broadcasts running.

Naturally, they dug into George's life, tracking down his ex-wife, daughter, and other relations who, to their credit, refused to comment. But George's Main Street neighbours stated how shocked they were and that he had always been quiet and polite.

However, one did say: "He was just a lonely old man."

George's former trucking company colleagues referred to him as a steady chap who never came late, and ex-classmates called him studious and a good sport.

They even found a former schoolteacher who-at 103-actually remembered George, saying he was a quiet boy with limited potential.

A Geriatric Psychologist, good on TV, labelled it a tragedy of our times and a telling statement on the isolation and despair the elderly often face, especially men.

But most of the media attention focused on George's fellow bus passengers, on-the-spot interviews with those sitting nearby, some of whom showed, then offered to sell their mobile phone footage. They said the older man had been mumbling about his Lincoln Continental and losing his driver's licence before shooting himself. They also said he had been talking to a Chinese girl who jumped off the bus and disappeared.

*

After leaving the bus, Debbie Chan had run north up Watson until reaching Broadway, where she entered a Vietnamese restaurant and managed to order a large bowl of soup with green tea. Still trembling from shock, she lowered her head to the table and wept uncontrollably, attracting some attention, but nobody tried to console her.

It took several minutes for Debbie to recover, and then she swallowed some soup and drank some tea. She wasn't sure where to go or what to do, but she had already missed her morning class, and there was no way she was going to work at the bakery. She needed someone to talk to, but she wasn't sure who.

Calling her stern parents was out of the question. They would only tell her to get a grip, and her two siblings were no better, too busy or distracted to listen to their sister.

Debbie took out her mobile and scanned the phone book, searching for the right person, finally settling on Violet Bouvier, whom she had met at Langara. Violet was a Métis from Northern Saskatchewan. She was twenty-eight, tall and stringy, and looked like she had lived. Violet was a student in Aboriginal Studies and took some science courses because she wanted to become a nurse.

"Hello. Violet."

"Who's this?"

"It's, ah, Debbie Chan. You know… I go to Langara."

"Oh, right. Debbie! Sorry. I didn't recognize your voice."

"That's all right," said Debbie.

"So, ah, what's up? You sound a bit weird."

"Yeah. Listen, Violet. Something horrible has just happened to me. Absolutely horrible. And, here, Debbie's voice broke, and she sobbed. "I really need someone to talk to."

There was a moment of silence. "Yeah. Okay. I understand. Where are you now?"

"I'm in a restaurant on Broadway and Watson."

"Okay. Look, Debbie. I live on Ontario near 14th. So, I'm close to where you are now. I'll give you the address, and you can come on over. Don't worry. It's no problem."

"Thank you, Violet."

Minutes later, Debbie, who was a fast walker, arrived at Violet's place. When the door opened, Debbie broke into tears, and Violet hugged her distraught classmate.

"Debbie," she cooed, patting her. "What the hell happened?"

"You won't believe it," explained Debbie, moving to Violet's couch.

"I was on a bus, and I offered my seat to an old man, but he was offended. Then he started to go on about a car he had owned. Then, he pulled out a gun and shot himself. Right in front of me."

"Jesus Christ," muttered Violet. "I just heard about that on the radio. They said that the bus was very crowded and that there was blood everywhere."

Debbie nodded. "I actually got some on my coat, but it rinsed off in the rain. I can't believe that this happened."

Again, Debbie began to weep, and Violet sat beside her and patted her shoulder. "It'll be okay, Debbie. You just have to let it pass. Believe me: it will."

"I can't believe it happened! I mean, when he first pulled out the gun, I thought he was going to kill me. Then he pointed the gun at his head, and I didn't know what to do. "

"It's not your fault, Debbie. You didn't do anything wrong. Obviously, the old guy had a few loose-screws."

"He was talking about how he had lost his driver's licence and how he had sold his car, and I didn't know what to say, so I just sat there."

"You probably did the right thing. But, no doubt, right now, you're in a state of shock. You need to recover. Try to focus on other things."

"That won't be easy," said Debbie Chan.

*

Joyce Patterson felt she had played her cards well.

After receiving the news of her father's suicide, she had quietly hung up, then poured herself a double rye and ginger, promptly followed by a single. After that, she had sat on the couch and cried before rising and strolling through her living room, sadly glancing at the photos on the mantelpiece. There was one of the whole family, meaning Joyce, her two sons, and her parents. One of her and her parents and one of her parents together, then apart. The last one had been taken after their divorce when they were in their early seventies. Mum had left because he was boring and cranky, and ignorance had never stopped him from having strong opinions. Still, he hadn't been a bad father. Mostly mediocre with some wonderful and terrible moments mixed in. He had always been there when it mattered.

Joyce took the photo of her dad off the mantelpiece and sat on the sofa, holding it tightly, almost cradling it, as it were frail and weak like a baby or an older person. Don't blame yourself, she thought. You didn't kill him.

It wasn't until two hours later that Joyce finally called her son Robert, who still lived in Vancouver.

"Hi, mum."

"Hi, Robert."

"What's up?"

"Robert, I have some terrible news."

"Oh, no. What happened?"

"A couple of hours ago, I got a call from the Vancouver police. Your grandfather shot himself on a city bus."

"What?"

"Apparently, he got on the bus, started mumbling, and then pulled out a gun and killed himself. At least that's what the police said."

"Jesus Christ!'

Joyce sighed. "I know it sounds unbelievable, but that's what the police said, and no doubt it's true. So anyway, your grandfather is dead, and that's that."

"I guess so. Anyway, are you okay?"

"As well as can be expected. I've had a couple of drinks, but I'm still pretty steady. "

"Would you like me to come over?"
Joyce thought about it. "Yeah. If you could, that would be great, but first I was hoping you could call a few people? It has to be done, and I'm really not sure I'm up to it."

"Sure, mum. No problem."

"Thanks. First of all, call your brother."

"Sure."

"Then your grandmother Patterson. "

"All right."

"And phone your cousins Janet and Bob."

"I'll do that."

"Thanks. And please ask them not to speak to the press. I want to keep this as low-key as possible. The less publicity, the better."

"I understand, mum. I'll try to call them, and then I'll come right over."

"Thank you, Robert. Thanks a lot."

*

Joyce sent her father's body to an undetaker's where it was cremated, the ashes placed in a large grey urn. After that, she quietly waited for the fuss to die down.

November became December, the weather cooler, the rain as relentless as ever. George had been dead for three weeks, and his remains were still at the funeral parlour. Finally, a full month after his death, a discreet obituary was put in the local papers, informing readers that the funeral would be held at St. John's Anglican Church (Church of England) at three in the afternoon. Mourners were asked not to buy flowers but to forward a cheque to the Canadian Suicide Prevention Society, which some did.

*

Canon Philip Edwards was almost the perfect Anglican vicar. Tallish, grey-haired, thin, he spoke with a soft Cornish accent and had a Master's in psychology. For many years, he had been a social worker, and it was often said that he had a human touch, which meant his small congregation was loyal but unfortunately shrinking due to death and demographics.

Canon Edwards was good at funerals, adept at expressing sympathy and dealing with the bereaved, and he did his utmost for George

Patterson's family. Told it would be a small funeral-perhaps fifteen people-he prepared to welcome family members, most of whom would be nieces, nephews, or grandchildren. George Patterson's ex-wife was not expected to attend, which was sad, but at least the deceased was not leaving a heartbroken widow. Unfortunately, Canon Edwards had seen too many of those.

There would be a short service, then a quick trip to an East Vancouver cemetery where George Patterson's ashes would be laid to rest. Following that, there would be a light lunch at George's Main Street house, and that would be it. Not all the mourners were expected to attend.

*

Since the bus suicide, Debbie Chan had not been herself. Instead, she cried frequently and was unable to sleep, tormented by terrible, eery nightmares of the old man glaring at her, then pointing the gun and killing himself.

At Langara College, she had begun counselling, sobbing encounters where she spilled her guts, and the psychologist just listened, then told her it would pass.

But her grades were starting to suffer, and at the bakery, she had received a stern warning about her job performance.

Fortunately, Violet had been a great comfort, spending time with Debbie and doing her best to keep Debbie occupied, though it baffled Violet that the bus suicide had had such an impact.

"You need to put this behind you," advised Violet. "Somehow, you have to move on."

"I need closure," replied Debbie. "Someway, I have to find closure.

Still, closure was hard to come by, and Debbie continued scanning the media for remnants of the bus suicide, but it was now as dead as George Patterson, who had been a three-day wonder.

Acknowledgements –

Richard Beamish
April 30, 1953 to December 8, 2020

Kempton Dexter is honoured to assist Ron in compiling <u>Guy Stories</u>, written by their old and mutual friend, Richard Beamish. Be it writer, musician or visual artist, Kempton is an advocate of the DIY tradition. "Grandpa Dex" currently lives in Esquimalt, B.C. His own most recent collection of short stories is <u>Paris of the Pacific Northwest</u> (2021).

Ron Kearse lists travelling, photography, art, reading and history as his primary sources of inspiration. An artist, broadcaster, actor, and writer, Ron has a colourful and varied work résumé. Having lived a nomadic life, Ron has settled in Victoria, British Columbia, with his partner James.

157